THE COSMOLOGY OF BING

THE COSMOLOGY OF BING

by

Mitch Cullin

THE PERMANENT PRESS
SAG HARBOR, NY 11963

© 2001 by Mitch Cullin

Library of Congress Cataloging-in-Publication Data

Cullin, Mitch
    The Cosmoglogy of Bing: a novel / by Mitch Cullin
      p. cm.
    ISBN 1-57962-030-2 (alk. paper)
    1. College teachers--Fiction. 2. College students--Fiction.
    3. Houston (Tex)--Fiction. 4. Alcoholics--Fiction. I. Fiction.

PS3553.U2955 C67 2001
813'.6--dc21   00-064253
                                        CIP

THE PERMANENT PRESS
4170 Noyac Road
Sag Harbor, NY 11963

for Peter Chang,
and for Robert Drake

Several chapters of the text were previously published, in slightly different form, by Alyson Books (*Circa 2000: Gay Fiction at the Millennium*)—to the editors and publisher I extend my deepest gratitude for their belief in this book.

Thanks to the following for support, inspiration, and invaluable information: John D. Barrow (*The Origin of the Universe*—Basic Books), Diane Breier, Peter Chang, sisters Charise and Chay and the girls, Barbara Cooper, Paul Davies (*The Last Three Minutes*—Basic Books), F & Z & Y, Mary Gaitskill, Amon Haruta, Jemma, godson Jesiah, Donald Judd (*Complete Writings: 1975-1986*—Van Abbemuseum), Tom Lavoie, Alfred K. Mann (*Shadow of a Star*—Freeman), Martin and Judith, Mom and Mike, John Nichols, Bill Oberdick, A. Chad Piper, Robert Phillips (*In Praise of my Prostate*), Charlotte Roybal, brother Steve, Joe Strummer, Terry Wolverton—and the Chairmen of the Board: Brad Thompson and my father Charles Cullin.

It's only the singing of the stars, that burnt out a long time ago. —David Byrne, "A Long Time Ago"

Oh love is the crooked thing,
There is nobody wise enough
To find out all that is in it,
For he would be thinking of love
Till the stars had run away,
And the shadows eaten the moon.
          —W.B. Yeats, *The Young Man's Song*

PROLOGUE

THANK GOD *for the dry martini served during lunch.*

Thank God for the whisky sour once the plates were removed from the table, and a second whisky sour before escaping, thank you very much.

Then how lovely the world seemed to Bing when he exited Eric's Rotisserie and began walking across campus, not at all drunk, no, not even tipsy. At last the fall faculty luncheon was finished, so now he ambled forward, already late for his Thursday afternoon class, leaving the others behind—his associates in the Astronomy Department, that cloistered threesome of Dr. Turman, Dr. Rosenthal, Dr. McDouglas, or, as he often denounced them to his wife, that Holy Trinity of Rot: "The faggot, Jew, and royal cunt." The summer break hadn't changed their minds one bit; they despised him for no other reason, he imagined, than for just being himself—surely outspoken (yes, yes, after a couple of drinks it was hard to stop talking), sometimes irreverent (a few humorous remarks here and there at his colleagues' expense), a cosmologist obsessed by the apocalyptic possibility of vacuum decay (the annihilation of everything, instant crunch, space-time reduced to a sudden singularity)—but, with oaks branching out overhead, shading the sidewalk, he could care less. Why bother? He had tenure, a book on supernovae in its third printing, the respect of three or four graduate students, the admiration of earnest undergraduates. The Holy Trinity couldn't disgrace him even if they tried. And did they try? Had they?

Almost a year ago Dr. Turman, the department head, had mentioned complaints received from several students— one ludicrous charge involving flatulence and sexist jokes, another depicting Bing, disheveled and seemingly intoxicated, staggering about a classroom, making sloppy notations on the chalkboard.

"All fabrications," Bing insisted. "Lies of the worst kind."
He knew damn well that he never behaved in such ways.
"If I had, believe me, I'd remember."
Nonetheless, he was warned.

"Put your house in order," Dr. Turman said, that contemptible queen. "This reflects badly on all of us, and you'd better pray I don't catch you plastered on campus."

The following spring, a potentially damaging complaint was filed. But it didn't come from a student. Joy Vanderhoof, the administrative secretary for the department, claimed Bing called in the middle of night, twice in March, and screamed obscenities at her—"You vile cow! Repugnant excrement! Judas lover!"

Her written grievance stated: He was obviously drunk. To be honest, I had a difficult time understanding him. He said I was evil. He said I should be ashamed of myself. When I asked why, he started yelling. So I hung up. When he called two weeks later, our conversation was pretty much the same, except I hung up quickly rather than allowing him the opportunity to yell.

Once again, Bing protested his innocence in Dr. Turman's office. He rose from his chair and paced, saying, "Where's the evidence? There isn't any, right? The woman was most likely dreaming, or under the influence. Or both. She's deluded, Mike. And she's vicious. She has it in for me. I think you do too."

"That's nonsense. You know it. But come on, Bing, you can't help wondering why she'd lie about this. Frankly, I don't think she would. Do you?"

"I have no idea. I really don't."

But, in reality, he understood everything. Joy Vanderhoof hated him because Dr. McDouglas hated him. Dr. McDouglas hated him because, as she put it, "He lacked professionalism and style." When he said hello, she ignored him. When he spoke in meetings, she frowned. So did Joy. How cozy those two hens were, with their wide hips and cups of coffee, gossiping in the lounge like catty school-girls. He'd overheard them, stood outside the lounge and eavesdropped. They were talking about him, whispering and laughing. And what had Joy said about his wife? What was it again?

"Pitiful thing, she belongs in that movie, you know, What Ever Happened to Baby Jane?"

"But she's scarier."

"Oh, that's awful. We're bad."

Then Joy laughed. She laughed so loudly that it startled Bing.

Evil, he thought. I hope you die pleading.

And for a moment he considered surprising them. He'd stride into the lounge, pointing a shaky finger, saying nothing—leveling them with an accusatory glare. Instead, he turned and walked away, mumbling, "Rotten bitches, rotten—"

So perhaps he did call Joy. Perhaps he wanted to put her straight, to wake her from her smug sleep and rattle her. Anyway, she couldn't prove it. She never did. Still, Bing was warned, though less sternly than before ("If you didn't call her, I'm truly sorry. If you did and it comes to light, there'll be serious consequences."), and he wore his indignation for weeks afterwards, shaking his head and scowling when Joy was nearby. In some small sense, he figured, it was a victory.

But now, this fall, the Holy Trinity struck back. He was assigned only one section to teach, a simple overview class for undergrads—Origins of the Universe, Tuesdays and Thursdays, 1:20-2:35 p.m., ASTR 305G; a demotion of sorts, no doubt pursued by fat-ass McDouglas, agreed upon by Rosenthal, okayed by Turman. Ignoring past protocol, he hadn't been consulted on the decision. Furthermore, he had always worked with both the brightest graduates and smartest undergraduates, had taught two co-convening courses each semester (Cosmology and Astrophysics in the *fall, Theoretical Astrophysics and Theories of Space-Time in the spring).*

"It's unfair, Mike. I might as well be a part-time lecturer."

"That's ridiculous. You're getting more freedom than the rest of us and your salary is the same. Christ, you go on and on about never having enough hours in the week for research—so you've finally got it. I'm envious. Who wouldn't be?"

"That's not the point."

So what was?

He wouldn't say.

But Dr. Turman knew—Rosenthal was teaching Astrophysics, McDouglas was doing Cosmology. And Bing, paranoid and worried Bing, his lot was the Origins of the Universe and restless undergrads and attendance taken at every lecture and extensive homework assignments and sloppy term papers and quizzes and exams and boring office hours when he had better things to do. Naturally, a man of Bing's position would feel somewhat slighted, a man who had spent sixteen years engaging intense undergrads from the Honors Program and often brilliant graduate students. But there was a drinking problem to contend with, complicated by increasingly erratic behavior (public flatulence being one thing, harassing phone calls being quite another). Poor Bing, he really wasn't the envy of anyone.

"You're taking this too personally."

"Exactly how should I take it then?"

"I suppose, well, as a gift."

A gift. That was funny.

No matter, Bing thought. You can't humiliate me so easily. I'll take your gift and make the most of it. You'll see.

And here on a humid August afternoon, while the city of Houston waited for autumn, Bing found himself smiling. Moss University was teeming with fresh faces, and he felt uncanny and sharp, as new and alive as the young people passing him on the sidewalk. With his thinning gray hair combed neatly, swept over the bald spot on his shiny scalp, his bow tie pressing at his throat, he strode without haste— the very vision of a self-assured and purposeful academic— studying those who came toward him, on their way to and from classes.

The undergrads were obvious. Backpack straps pulled around shoulders, hands in pockets or arms cradling books. Such serious expressions. Boys with baseball caps, T-shirts and ridiculous baggy jeans. Girls in jeans and T-shirts, not so different in attire from the boys. All crossing the open quad, moving beneath Herbert R. Moss' stern statue, a towering monument to the university founder whose grave existed below the marble cowboy boots of his likeness.

Moss, Bing thought, you look miserable. Buck up, old man, there they are, enriching themselves at the finest private university in Texas; the future you spoke so passionately about: "Souls not yet born, let them be free to consider everything when they come here, where no possibility or dream shall be denied." Indeed. But times change, of course, and your pastoral institution is hardly pastoral anymore, flourishing instead amongst skyscrapers and traffic. And, yes, sidewalks weren't part of your grand plan, just grass and trees, a mingling of nature and stately halls. Unfortunate, I know, that a few souls not yet born would come into this world needing wheelchairs and easy access. Oh well. Anyway, I think your misery is really disdain; something about the young women traversing what was never meant to be theirs in the first place, denying a major part of your dream. You had no idea, did you?

Still, the young men remained plentiful. How perfect each one appeared, how contained; the best of them were lanky and immature, with their short hair and earrings, boxers showing past the waistline (casualness and vogue, that odd charm). They roamed in various directions, off to the library, heading for walkways that ran alongside red-

brick, ivy-covered buildings, a few pausing in the shade of oaks. Smooth skin and tanned necks sheltered under clustered leaves. Bing gazed at them as if he were staring through a telescope, aroused by a unique and revelatory discovery.

Was I ever like that?

The sun cast his shadow in front of him, giving his chubby and stunted limbs the illusion of wiry length. Forty years earlier, he was sprightly and vigorous, a swimmer for his college. Young men were his closest friends then. He showered in the locker room with them, got drunk with them, stayed awake until dawn smoking Lucky Strikes and listening to jazz records or reading poetry with them. And, how strange it seemed to him now, he was actually one of those handsome boys.

Except he was a Bing. He had always been. The name was a bad investment, bestowed upon him when Bing Crosby embodied American suaveness. His mother felt positive that Bings would someday rival Mikes. Only later, during his graduate years in the '60s, did the name become a joke, though he took any chiding in stride. To at least three professors he was The Big Bing, a student of infinite ideas and inexhaustible energy. To several peers, he was Bing Nothing—one who couldn't be stirred by student protests and politics and rock 'n' roll, not while stars exploded in supernovae and dispersed into space.

But these days, to his students and colleagues, what was he? A runty man, aged fifty-eight, who could easily pass for sixty-eight. And what did the mirror reveal? Someone far removed from the slender swimmer and his long dead namesake. More like W.C. Fields—the round face, fleshy and pale, the gin blossom nose and squinting eyes. Yes, he was The Bigger Bing, expanding at a steady rate, intrinsically the same, unbridled by time.

He checked his wristwatch.

Almost ten minutes late. And shit, he'd forgotten the

course notes in his office. No problem. The Origins of the Universe could be addressed without written aid.

And taking a deep breath, he continued forward, bringing a palm to his scalp, patting down renegade hairs. There would be no more stories of a disarranged and drunken Bing. He'd surprise those cryptos—damnable Turman, Rosenthal, McDouglas. Sneaky Joy Vanderhoof.

That's right, he thought. You can't humble me that easy. I'm bigger than you think.

FALL

BING

1.

Damn notes, Bing thought. Should've kept them in a pocket.

And where had they left off? What was said? He couldn't recall having even lectured. The syllabuses were passed out, surely. Introductions were made, of course. But today—where to begin? He had no idea.

"Well, let me see. Perhaps I should ask you. I suspect some fledgling astronomers in the room have a few thoughts on how to proceed."

This was the Thursday class, supposedly the same students as from the Tuesday class, yet Bing found himself standing in front of quiet strangers—sixty-eight blank faces staring at him, slouched bodies occupying seats in the Thompson Planetarium, not a single person worth remembering. But the first weeks always seemed awkward, a required adjustment period while minds were being made up (some students would drop the course, latecomers would appear). And sometimes a month passed before a class formed its own distinct personality—morose, cheerful, maybe chatty—and from that collective one or two promising individuals usually emerged.

"Professor Owen, can I ask a question?"

A young woman's voice, very deep and loud. But she hadn't raised her hand. So Bing peered forward, looking for her, and said, "You just did. Ask another if you wish."

No one smiled or laughed. A tough crowd.

"Stand up please. I don't know where you are."

She cleared her throat and then stood, a solitary soul in the back row.

"There you are," he said.

Yes, there she was. Bleached hair as white as milk, cropped close to her scalp. Black tank top. Fingers fidgeting with the loops of her blue jeans.

"This might be off the subject, but I was wondering if you believed in alien life, as in extraterrestrial beings visiting us. Because I do. I mean, if you consider that we all come from the same source then it doesn't seem so impossible that equally intelligent beings or even smarter-than-us beings might actually be here from another galaxy. Because when I was fourteen my brother and me actually saw what was obviously an alien craft one night at my grandparents' house in Virginia. There's no other explanation, really. So I'm not surprised at all."

Sit down, he thought. Go away. Die.

Blank faces turned to see her. Then, as if on cue, the very same faces returned to Bing, who was rubbing his chin. Chewing absently on the cap of his pen, a boy sitting in the front row smirked and shook his head. Bing liked that kid.

"There was a question somewhere in there, I think."

"Yes."

"Seems you want to know if I believe extraterrestrials visit the earth?"

She nodded.

"Something like that, yeah."

"But you already know they do. I'll just take your word for it."

He glanced at the boy in the front row, giving him a wink.

"Well, I guess I was wondering if you feel our government has been lying to us about—"

He knew her. He had known her for years and years. Sometimes she was male, sometimes black, sometimes Latino or Asian, more often than not she was female and white and young. And she had to be heard. He had never taught a class in which she didn't exist. And when her peers

22

grew tired of her rambling—her inane questions and comments—she would still fail to sense the complete meaninglessness of her own words and thoughts. White-girl disease, he called it. How she talked talked talked, blathering with authority. He hated her with every inch of his flesh.

"Hitler's mother," Bing said, interrupting her.

That got their attention.

One hundred and thirty-six eyes gazed at him beneath the starless planetarium sky, indifference now tinged with curiosity. This was Origins of the Universe? No Big Bang. No expansion of space. Wasn't Professor Owen supposed to inflate a balloon—a balloon that represents galaxy clusters—explaining that the space between the clusters increases, but the size of the clusters doesn't?

"Hitler's mother had a saying. She'd go, 'If you believe it, it is so.' Unfortunately, her son took that to heart. Anyway—and what I suppose I'm trying to say is—if you believe it, dear, it is so. Frankly, this whole extraterrestrial thing leaves me limp."

And that was that.

"Okay."

She shrugged, sinking into her seat.

But what he wanted to tell her was that the universe was rich with tangible mysteries. Honestly, no aliens need apply. And in our galaxy—where vast storms rotated counterclockwise on Neptune, and ice volcanoes shot frigid geysers on Triton, and the sun's magnetic activity inexplicably waned and intensified again every eleven years—there was profound violence and beauty. That's what I should tell you, he thought, but I won't. I'm bored and restless and I don't want to be here any more than the rest of you do. So I'm sorry. My notes are in my office; that's where I'll be going. I thought we could manage without them. I guess not. Some days are better than others, I suppose.

What now?

He consulted his watch.

Over ten minutes late in arriving. Then about ten minutes of engaging zombie children, a brief discussion concerning aliens in Virginia and government cover-ups. Approximately fifty minutes remaining.

Class dismissed.

"Do your reading or readings. Do whatever the syllabus says to do. Be ready on Tuesday, all right? Have a great weekend. Do yourself a favor—have a super weekend!"

And Bing watched them all rise from their seats en masse, gathering books and backpacks. The pen-chewing boy shuffled by without as much as a nod. No one said a word, at least not to him; they filed out through the side doors, making a hasty escape— quiet as church mice, just the sounds of big jeans swooshing, sneakers clomping, the doors opening and shutting.

Then he was alone.

How long had it taken? Thirty seconds? Maybe fifteen? He hadn't noticed White Girl Disease leaving, but, thank God, she was nowhere to be seen.

You keep haunting me, he thought. You're a ghost. Good riddance.

And just then, how peaceful the planetarium felt; this was the only decent place in Houston for watching the stars. At night the city glowed, eclipsing the heavens. But in here—with the flip of a switch, the twisting of a few knobs—the city disappeared, the Milky Way shone clear and perfect; one could almost imagine sitting in the countryside after nightfall, an unclouded sky above, the constellations revealing themselves.

As a college student, Bing worked at a similar place, though it was smaller and in disrepair. He ran the Star Show for high school field trips, putting on elaborate displays while selections from Holst's *The Planets* played through a single loudspeaker. The ceiling leaked, the dome interior was streaked with water damage. But when the lights dimmed and the stars faded in, the ruin became invisible.

"This is where you find your spot in the galaxy," he would explain to his audience. "My role is to guide you along."

At eighteen, he wasn't much older than most of the field trippers. Still, he sensed that he was further along, that he'd digested vast amounts of knowledge in a short period of time. He ate textbooks.

"I'm probably a genius," he told his mother.

"You're a genius of something," she'd reply, "except I don't know what."

It was 1958, and he studied under Professor Graham Wilmot, a teacher whose lectures made Bing fall in love with the universe.

"That's why you're here," Wilmot told his students, "to find your place in the universe. My function is to help you."

And he did; it was Wilmot who offered Bing the job of running the Star Show, and it was Wilmot who wrote him a flattering recommendation when it came time to apply for graduate school. But the Star Show—listening to Holst, running the projector, speaking to a group of high schoolers as if he were a professor—that was the best. He couldn't thank Wilmot enough.

And some evenings, after swimming practice, he unlocked the planetarium, snuck inside, and performed a Star Show for his own enjoyment. And more than once, when the occasion presented itself, he brought someone along with him in the middle of the night, a man he'd met at a bar near campus. A stranger. Romantic, not sleazy, he reasoned. A discreet encounter, a mutual exchange. The chance of discovery was slim. Forget that he never knew the man's name, or that he felt miserable for days afterwards. How many ended up going with him? As a freshman, six. As a sophomore, nine. None as a junior—that's when he began dating his future wife. Never again, he promised himself. I'm a new man, I'm changed.

That was forty years ago.

2.

THE COURSE notes—or, in the very least, the syllabus. One or the other would be helpful.

"Dammit, where are you?"

Bing leaned forward in his seat and began rummaging through the papers on his desk, exploring a mess of unread memos, forgotten letters, a year's worth of university bulletins that he was supposed to give students.

Not there.

He lifted books. He checked inside his briefcase, twice.

Nothing.

Think.

He propped his elbows among the papers, cupping his face in his hands.

Let's see, let's see. That's right, yes. Must be at home. Somewhere on his desk at home. Of course.

"Hey, did you get Tong's e-mail?"

Who's that?

His hands parted as if fastened to hinges. Peekaboo.

There was Casey, filling the office doorway with his girth, his Metallica concert shirt, his bushy topknot of hair (an obscene tuft that sprouted from his crown like a pom-pom); he grinned within his woolly beard. "Dr. Spacey Casey," Bing sometimes called him, but only after several rounds at their favorite pub, The Stag's Horn.

"Haven't checked my e-mail today," Bing said. "I'll do it later."

"Well, I suggest you do it sooner rather than later. He's got big news."

"I know that. He woke me with the news, so I know. I knew before the rest of you bastards did. Tong and me are like this—"

Bing crossed his fingers—left hand, right hand—holding them up for Casey to see.

"Yeah, yeah, whatever—pretty interesting, no?"

"Yes," Bing said, "it's amazing."

It was worth envy; on an extended sabbatical in southwestern Texas, atop a mountain peak, Professor Tong had left his night watch at the McDonald Observatory and walked outside. He was hoping to confirm with his eyes what had already been revealed by a freshly developed photograph—a photograph taken through the telescope two hours previously. And while searching the sky, he spotted the luminous object, an anomaly which hadn't existed earlier that evening, glowing amid a satellite galaxy of the Milky Way. Making sure astronomers worldwide would know, Tong reported the sighting to the International Astronomical Union. Then he called Bing the following morning, waking him with the words, "A supernova. Ostensibly it is, but I'm positive. Without a doubt in my mind, a fifth-magnitude object. I saw it. Didn't even need the telescope. It was there, plain as day."

Plain as night, Bing thought. Lucky sonofabitch.

"The little guy sounded loopy," he told Casey. "Thought he was drunk at first."

"Hell, I'd be drunk," said Casey. "I'd start drinking at dawn and keep going. I mean, Jesus, you remember the last time a supernova got seen with the naked eye?"

"Not in my lifetime."

"For certain. And you know it ain't happening again while either of us is still breathing. Tong just made the books."

The books, history, being in the right place at the right time—what did it matter?

"I'm happy for him," Bing said.

Casey flexed his shoulders.

"I'd love to say the same."

Bing thought: I'm sure you would, Casey. But all's fair, and you're a part-time lecturer. Men like you don't make the books. Men like Tong and me do.

That was why they were professors, that's why they got

sabbaticals and research grants—so they could make the books. So they could write them too. And why exactly wasn't Casey at the faculty luncheon anyway? Bing could've used his company. No one had talked to him. Well, almost no one. The Holy Trinity sure didn't. Not for a second. But if Casey and Tong had been there with him, they could've had their own trinity—then they could've walked out together into the fine afternoon, laughing and talking like great friends. There are some things more important than supernovae, Bing thought, and friendship is one of them. And love. And a good joke. Which reminds me. Did you hear McDouglas is getting liposuction? The operation takes place May, June, July, August, September, October, November and December. That's a good one. I need to tell you that sometime. I think you'd like it. Tong would.

He motioned for Casey to enter. Then he pointed at the chair in front of his desk.

"Come and sit a spell. I've got office hours soon, don't think anyone will show up though."

"Would like to," said Casey, scratching the tip of his nose with a finger, "except my three o'clock class would probably miss me. How about drinks later? The Stag's Horn and happy hour?"

"Can't tonight. Tomorrow's better. Is that good for you?"

"Sure. I'll call you at home."

"Sounds good."

Bing nodded. A resolute nod, like a firm handshake. And after Casey wandered away into the corridor, he went to the door and closed it, locked it, tested the handle making certain.

Just for a moment, he thought. Just while I get a nip.

The nip. Ten High bourbon. A half-pint bottle, half full, in the bottom drawer of his file cabinet. Then a quick swig. One more. Go easy. That's enough, that's good. He returned the bottle, hiding it between manila folders, filing it under the letter T.

The drawer slid shut.

Bing sighed as he stood. He wiped his lips with the back of his hand. Then he straightened his bow tie, smoothed his hair, checked his zipper.

Ready.

He unlocked the door and pulled it open.

And waiting in the corridor, standing before the doorway, a green backpack hanging from a shoulder, was the pen-chewing boy; with a fist raised, poised for knocking, his presence startled Bing.

"What're you doing?"

"Sorry," the boy said, lowering his fist. "I was about to knock. You're having office hours, right?"

Bing's face revealed nothing.

"These are my office hours, yes."

The boy let the backpack slip; in one deft move the strap went from his shoulder to his hand, where the backpack then dangled at his side.

"There's this article you wrote. It interested me a lot."

Article? What article?

Bing glanced at the boy's slim, tanned neck. Then he glanced at his shoes, then at his blue eyes.

"You're in my class, correct?"

"Yes. I read an article you published in *Scientific Foundations.*"

"Which one?"

"'Vacuum Decay and Cosmic Locality.'"

"You read that? Really?"

Bing couldn't believe it—this child reading and understanding that article.

"Yes."

"You're an undergraduate?"

"Yes."

What an attractive boy he was too: tall and lanky, a born basketball player, with sandy hair parted in the middle, hair that fell into place after a hand ran through it. And how clean he seemed; his skin looked scrubbed and ruddy, his big swooshy jeans were pressed, his black tennis shoes unblemished. Yes, the hoop earring in his left nostril was silly, but, Bing reasoned, he's young. And smart. And handsome—the kind of boy who must be beautiful and toned and smooth without his clothing on. Perhaps a swimmer.

"Come in, please."

Then the door shut behind them, and Bing found himself seated at his desk, the boy sitting across from him. Between them the disarray of papers. And Bing wondered if the boy would like a pen to chew, but decided it might be an inappropriate suggestion, even if mentioned in jest. Anyway, this was business.

Name?

Nick. Nick Sulpy. A sophomore.

Major?

Undecided.

Except he loved reading, especially Whitman and Salinger. So maybe an English degree.

Bing wanted to know more about him. But not yet. Not today.

"And what exactly did you think of my article?"

Bing felt the Ten High in his throat, a residual sensation, warming.

Nick's face brightened. How thin his lips were, how red.

There are some things more important than supernovae, Tong. There are other worlds to explore with the naked eye, you know.

3.

Ms. Bunny was late. And Bing was worried.

"She's dead."

He'd braved a rainy evening and slick streets, had arrived early so he could get a stool beside the baby grand. Now he waited, sipping his second pink lady, wondering if Ms. Bunny met with tragedy en route to the piano bar. Maybe her car skidded from the wet road, crashing into a tree, the impact killing her. He imagined her fake eyelashes knocked askew, her bones cracking, her powder-blue wig flying through the windshield amid shattering glass, and then the confused expressions of the paramedics as they discovered that the enchanting Ms. Bunny was, in reality, a man.

No more tacky jokes and sad songs, Bing thought. No more "Stormy Weather." No more "That Old Black Magic." Ms. Bunny is no more.

The announcement of her death would create an astonished silence, shocking all the other men seated around the piano, the regulars for Torch Song Thursday at The Naked Brunch, those chatty old queens with their dyed hair and silk shirts and cocktails; there wasn't a jowly face among them worthy of consoling Bing. Only Damien. But Damien was different. He was younger than the rest—thirty-three, a psychology graduate student, favored as a research assistant—and cute in a compact elfish way: He'd made a living as a jockey before pursuing a doctorate.

And it pleased Bing to be seen in Damien's company. The pair turned heads when arriving together, aroused whispers when settling next to one another near the piano. They traded rounds like close friends, talked intimately like lovers, aware the whole time that they were being watched with a mixture of disgust and regard—*good God, it's them again, sugar daddy and his pretty boyfriend.*

31

"That's a horrendous notion," Damien said, patting Bing's hand. "Ms. Bunny isn't dead. She's getting ready."

"Suppose so."

Bing appreciated the pat, the open display of affection, and hoped the others had spotted it.

I won't be alone, he thought. If it's tragedy, then I'll have someone to support me as I leave. Someone to drive me home, to help me inside. I'm not like you sad sacks, not even close.

And perhaps Damien would hold him in the car. Would that be asking too much? Maybe a hug, or a kiss, or even—

Bing knew it was pointless. Once, while parked in front of The Naked Brunch, he'd leaned forward and kissed Damien on the cheek. Then he kissed his neck. And Damien didn't protest, gave no sign that he was bothered by this older man reaching under his shirt. But then he told Bing to stop; he said it was wrong, said that they were friends, just friends. And there was Bing's wife to think about.

"She won't know. No one will. Me and you only. Our secret. No one gets hurt."

"Someone always gets hurt."

"But if we're discreet, if we keep it to ourselves—"

"I'm sorry, Bing, but no. I'm sorry."

"Nothing to be sorry about," Bing said. "I understand."

So they'd be friends. Bing didn't care, as long as he could be associated with Damien. As long as those other queens thought otherwise. Every Thursday they'd go to The Naked Brunch, and, at the end of the evening, they'd shake hands. It didn't matter that they both shared and hid the same desires, or that they both loved show tunes and exotic drinks. Or that they had met by chance, not at school, not in the basement men's restroom at the library (a rumored hotbed of sexual activity), but at this piano bar. It just didn't matter.

Anyway, Damien lived with his mother. Bing had a wife. There was a quarter century age difference. Bing could be his father; he hated that idea. And there was another difference—Damien was obvious, effeminate, a bit prissy; Bing, as he imagined himself, was masculine, a real man, inclined only toward a slight weakness for other men. He wasn't a faggot like Dr. Turman (Turman who lisped when he lectured, who had a boyfriend named Jeffrey). He had always loved his wife, always—and sometimes he strayed. Sometimes he wanted to be held. That's all.

How long had it been?

He didn't want to think about it, though he couldn't stop himself: There was his wife, and then there was Marc. But that was long ago, and it was painful remembering. How the world was different once—there weren't dance clubs like now, those places where boys went and danced and sweated to techno music. There were discos, of course, but he'd been too old for even them. Still, he never felt sorry for himself because his youth was squandered on the heavens. No regrets. Well, at least not many. Damien, he thought, I wish I could tell you something about myself, because I did love someone like you. And I lost him too. But that's no one's business except my own.

Yet he was young with Marc, or younger. He felt younger. The boy had been twenty-four. Bing had been thirty-six (three years older than Damien was now). And Marc—he was a student, an afternoon distraction from work. Bing loved him for three months and then he was gone. But they drank pink ladies together. Except it wasn't Ms. Bunny—it was Sister Judy. And it wasn't Texas, it was New York. But, Bing thought, there are some things that should be kept with one's self. So he wouldn't tell Damien how long it'd been since he slept with another man. Or how badly he sometimes missed Marc. Or that sometimes he dreamed about the boy and couldn't quite recall exactly what he had looked like. So it was better not dwelling too much on the past. It was better to talk about the weather instead.

"My God, it's raining men! Hail Mary, hallelujah!"

Ms. Bunny appeared, working the bar as she always did, wandering from man to man, touching chins, brushing cheeks. Soon she'd be at the piano, singing in that throaty voice of hers. But jokes came first, then sad songs.

"It's a Viagra convention in here, seriously. Just kidding, darlings. I'm bad, I know. God bless Viagra, that's all I got to say. Really, that drug is like Disneyland, honestly. You wait two hours for a three minute ride."

Laughter.

"That's funny," Bing said as he lifted his drink.

Ms. Bunny sauntered between tables, blowing kisses and rolling her eyes.

"She's alive," Damien said.

"What?"

Bing leaned in, putting his shoulder against Damien's shoulder.

"I didn't catch what you said."

But Damien looked away, smiling at Ms. Bunny as she moved toward them.

"Nothing," Damien said. "It's nothing."

Nothing, Bing thought. Of course, nothing at all.

4.

THE AIR smelled of sewage, of waste stirred by the rain. Bing sloshed across the damp lawn, heading for the porch, staggering in the light drizzle. And this was how he brought himself inside—waving to Damien when his VW pulled away from the curb. Then wiping his shoes on the doormat (mustn't make a mess). Then fumbling with the keys (don't forget them in the lock). Then through the front door (don't slam it shut). Then up the stairs—go slow, don't trip, be careful, easy on that squeaky top step—and then, there he was, short of breath, tipsy, relieved to be standing in his world.

Home. Why did he hate leaving it? Dread returning to it? He didn't know. And when did one of the upstairs guest rooms become his bedroom? When was it agreed that the upstairs—with its own bathroom, its wet bar—would be his? The downstairs hers? She got the backyard, the garden. He got the French windows that opened to the balcony. At what point were these decisions made?

A flick of a switch illuminated the study. His bookcases. His couch. The coffee table. Beyond, in an alcove, was his office, his desk, his Frank Lloyd Wright table lamp, more bookcases, the stereo.

"Yes, home is where you hang yourself," he told Pussy, his gray tabby who was curled on the couch. He went to her and stroked her coat. "Isn't that right?" he said, cooing like she was a baby. "Pussy is a pretty girl."

She raised her head just a bit, one eye closed, letting him scratch her chin.

"Pussy loves daddy."

And below his shoes, beneath the rug and floor, down there in his wife Susan's world, the house was dark but not quiet. She was asleep with the TV on—he could hear it droning in her bedroom, a late night religious program filtering into her brain, protecting her from those nightmares where she was drowning under a frozen lake. In the morning they'd talk. She'd make breakfast, serving him toast and orange juice and scrambled eggs with green chili. Then she'd ask for money (a check if he had less than ten dollars on him), something for Brother Van Horn in Atlanta, or The Faith Ministries in Baton Rouge, or Helpful Blessings in Orlando. He'd give her whatever was in his wallet. She'd accept his offering without a thank you; her black eyes revealing naught—no promise of salvation, no hope for prayers to be answered—even as her fingers closed around the bills.

But now she slept. And her book was on his coffee table, that slim volume of poetry, published the same year they both started teaching (Astrophysics for him, English Literature for her), before her brain played its trick and ended her career. Even then there were little clues, foretelling stanzas, lost on him until later.

> *To be only what I am, floating,*
> *Carried somewhere else, transported*
> *From one end to the other;*
> *All my days are really the same*
> *With varying degrees of cold and cold.*

How could he have known?

And how strange it was when Marc (that afternoon distraction of so many years ago—that lover of poets, of Bing) once quoted her as they lay together after sex. She had already changed, had stopped writing and teaching, but the distraction spoke her words, making them sound somehow new and significant: "Our needful embrace, a reminder that we are alone within ourselves."

"That's Susan," Bing said, matter-of-factly. "That's my wife. You know that, right?"

Marc began speaking the words again, slyly, whispering them.

But Bing cut him off.

"Please don't. She's ill and it seems cruel."

Marc turned on his back, breathing heavyily through his nose for effect.

"You love her more than me?"

"I can't say. It's different. It's not the same thing."

"Isn't it?"

Marc folded his arms over his chest; his right leg scooted off the edge of the bed, his foot dropped to the floor. Then how uncomfortable that bed was, how suddenly useless. Yet, the following afternoon, it would become wanted—the single mattress with baby-blue sheets, existing in a low-rent apartment (Marc had given Bing a key, a coffee cup, a hanger for his jacket and slacks).

He touched Marc's neck with his fingertips.

"You don't understand what it's like. It's rather complicated. She's my wife."

Marc looked at Bing as if some terrible lie had been uttered.

"You love her. That's why you're here with me."

"Daddy is parched."

Bing wandered to the wet bar, and Pussy followed, rubbing and weaving between his ankles. He fixed a gin and Sprite, pouring the drink into a dirty glass that was stained with bourbon. Then he crossed to his office, clicked the stereo on, listening as static crackled from the speakers. His favorite classical station had signed off for the night. Still, he let the racket continue, preferring the bothersome hiss over the muffled rumble of his wife's TV. "It's the universe's song," he often told his students, when explaining electrostatic disturbances. And, while unlatching the French windows, that's what he told himself.

"Cosmic radiation in E," he said, enjoying the sound of his own voice.

Pussy meowed at his feet. She joined him on the balcony, where they both sniffed the foul air. At last the rain had quit. Glancing skyward, Bing saw the reflection of the city lights, the clouds above glowing with a pinkish hue. The constellations were up there somewhere, he knew, but even on clear nights it was impossible to stargaze in Houston; the city ate darkness within a thirty-mile radius— and Bing longed for the country, a farmhouse atop a hill, a year's supply of gin, a telescope, a landmark discovery bearing his name.

"Daddy hates Tong."

He nudged Pussy with his shoe. Then, shaking his head, sipping his drink, he imagined what moved beyond those clouds—Cassiopeia, the Winter Triangle, Tong's dying star.

"No, no, I don't. I don't hate him. I love Tong, Pussy. He's my friend."

I'm plastered, Bing thought. I'm wrecked.

To begrudge Tong was unjust. To despise the Trinity of Rot was noble. They were getting the better of him, and now he felt miserable. Sometimes he convinced himself that it didn't matter—the petty politics, the nasty gossip—that by ignoring the slights he could even the score. Other times he wanted to scream, to leave Houston and never return. But that's what they wanted him to do.

"Fuckers!"

His voice frightened Pussy, who poofed her tail and crouched. He lunged forward, pressing his waist against the railing, and threw his glass down into the backyard.

"Someone cares," he said. "Someone cares."

He stepped away from the railing, taking a deep breath. Then he knelt—calming Pussy with his fingers, caressing her ears—and a strange notion slowly filled him, a notion that had taken time to surface. He started whistling, sensing the lessening of his mood, the righteousness of having been wronged, the desire for equity, the unexpected realization that moments ago seemed distant.

Someone cares.

What was his name? Like Marc. No, Mick. No, Nick. Nick. With a fondness for Whitman. Not a poet though, or an astronomer. But he'd read Bing's paper, was curious about vacuum decay. Bing would show the Trinity that they could only do so much; they couldn't prevent a teacher from engaging a student, or the creation of an independent study (if Nick was interested). How easy it would be, how simple. Origins of the Universe would become secondary. Vacuum Decay and Cosmic Locality would be the important class—just him and one student. It was perfect.

He lifted Pussy, cradling her. The same instant, he felt rain on his brow and nose. A thick mist began spraying the balcony. The cat, startled by the moisture on her coat, attempted to jump from Bing's arms, but he gripped her tightly, clutching her at his chest.

"There, there," he said, as her claws fastened into his jacket.

A thunderclap erupted—the static surged from the speakers—and Pussy struggled, emitting a tragic growl.

"There, there."

Bing shut his eyes for a moment, and made a wish. The same wish he made most nights: Remember everything tomorrow. Don't forget.

"Don't let me forget."

Then he released his hold, allowing Pussy to escape. But he remained for a while outside, swaying in the whirl of mist, as water cascaded down his face, licking his lips like a thirsty fool. At the piddliest hour of the night, he was the only man in the city praying for a flood.

SUSAN

5.

If a storm could sink the house
you would rather drown in your bed
than be saved by a man such as mine.
Yet stubbornness has shaped me,
is my resolve for affection untended,
like the soft palm that folds in upon the fly,
corralling the troublesome creature,
rather than crushing or setting him loose;
so he is mine as I remain his.

On our honeymoon night we only slept
and never stirred in those satin sheets
to grasp at the other's body: two lovers
choosing instead an expensive rest
before going forever from that suite.
So there was no virginal consummation,
for we had done away with that rite
months prior to the auspicious wedding,
which, like our sex, was haphazard
and colorless, a drawn out occasion.

And what do I know of passion now
that would ring honest and correct
as the very notion is a yawning breath
I'd prefer to exhale than possess?
Harder still to become dogged
with a love that seems pointless;
how not unlike seeking redemption
from one who has murdered a child.
Harder even to look right into the face

of a fly disrupting the tranquil home
where every surface is touched
by his large and stout body;
all was perfect and tidy there,
and yet bothersome legs
were keen on putting an unseen taint
in the rooms that a family should covet.
So all would be touched and bothered,
but when the fly landed in a woman's palm,
her smooth skin curled and wrinkled,
slowly enclosing him, keeping him there
as a strange and tickling problem;
this is what I know of our allurement,
his and mine.

NICK

6.

RETURNING FROM dinner, Nick found a yellow Post-It note stuck on his dorm room door, the words having been written as tiny and neat as possible: *Stranger, don't even think about entering this here abode . . . 'cuz . . . important meeting in the quad at 6 requires that <u>ONE OF US</u> be there, k? P.C. stuff, yadda yadda yadda. Don't miss out, or else! Me got work to do, but might make it in time. If not, fill I in. Look for me anyway, The Shadow.*

P.C. stuff? Important meeting?

Nick read the note again, trying to make some sense of it. He was Stranger, of course. That was his nickname. His roommate Takashi was The Shadow. But—

Shit, Nick thought. Right.

He tucked the note in his pocket. Then he looked at his watch. Seven past six. The Pi Crusters were plotting. Plans were being made without him. Turning on the heels of his sneakers, his backpack swinging in one hand, he bounded down the hallway, clomping wildly across carpet—then outside, but not before almost colliding with a pair of jocks who were entering the building.

"Hey!" and, "Asshole, watch it!"

"Sorry!"

Finally, there he was, picking up speed, sprinting along a walkway, heading toward the quad at dusk. He relished the early evening, how the heat of the day was cooled by a light breeze, how the chatter of birds replaced the busy shuffling of fellow students. Like the long-distance runner he'd been in high school, Nick fell into a proper gait. Right foot, left foot. Keep the breathing steady, find the rhythm. His stepfather had coached him, had warned him about overexertion: don't quit when the first wave of fatigue hits; push the body, keep pushing forward. The fatigue will disappear. (Thanks, Dad—good advice for a boy who wants to run as far away as possible.) But the desire to run for miles was no longer with him—at Moss University it seemed needless—and when reaching the quad he slowed, preferring instead to jog off the walkway, going where his sneakers pressed gently upon grass.

He checked his watch. Eleven past six.

Hurry. Go faster.

Up ahead was the meeting, well under way, and as Nick drew closer he noticed a smattering of Pi Crusters—some sprawled on their sides, most cross-legged—beneath a large oak, forming a haphazard circle around Debra and Bill (the brains behind the group and self-appointed Chief Creamers); what began three years previously as a simple prank—two undergraduate math majors intent on hurling coconut cream at the face of their bothersome department head—had blossomed into instant tradition. Soon Debra and Bill's targets became more ambitious, less personal, the goal being to humiliate those with narrow character and an inflated ego: the entire ROTC (four guys, one girl), a visiting Nation of Islam leader who called for a black revolution in which "white blood would fill the streets," the president of Campus Crusade for Christ, the dean (pied four times in one year), a feminist English professor outraged by "the sick bias for teaching patriarchal literature" at the university, and two separate commencement speakers (one a Nobel Prize-winning writer, the other a high-profile lawyer). Now thirty-six months after its inception, the popular and notorious Crusters totaled nearly fifty members, students drawn from all disciplines, each sworn to secrecy by a brief oath ("If I confess the pie, I get the pie!").

But the evening's turnout was meager, with only ten or so members, lounging in ragged fashion, listening while the Chief Creamers took turns speaking. No sooner had Nick joined the circle, stretching on his side and reclining against his backpack, when Bill said in that lazy West Texas drawl of his, "Okay, so let's meet a week from tonight, same time, same place, and we'll vote on potential pieheads."

"Don't be too obvious in your choices," Debra added. "Be creative. Let's give the Christians and the dean a break."

"Good point. All right, folks, see y'all next week then."

That was it? The meeting was over?

Thirteen past six.

Everyone climbed from the grass, dispersing in different directions, fanning out into the quad. Hoisting his backpack, Nick felt annoyed. He'd run for nothing, had nearly toppled a pair of jocks, had caught the last seconds of what appeared to be a very mundane meeting. Now he wondered what The Shadow was doing that kept him from attending. Not working, he thought. Anything but work. I know you, Tak.

"Where's your buddy?"

Bill draped an arm over Nick's shoulders; his breath smelt of beer. The eyes were bloodshot, unfocused.

"Don't know. Working, I guess."

"Homeworking, or working working?"

"Probably homeworking."

"That's a shame. Well, when you see him, tell him we need some good pieheads for next week's vote, right?"

"Sure thing."

Bill's arm slid away.

"You're a keeper, Nick."

He patted Nick's neck, then walked on, hobbling bowlegged after Debra. Nick watched him go, amazed that Bill—with his Wranglers and Stetson, his kicker boots, the Skoal can bulging in a pocket—could be a math major, let alone an assassin. Then Bill was next to Debra, reaching for her, pulling her close, giving her chin a sloppy kiss. Just as Nick started to leave, as he was about to trudge forward imagining Bill and Debra in bed together (whipped cream and cherries and sticky sticky sex), palms reached around his head, covering his eyes, stopping him.

"Hi, Stranger. Guess who?"

Then giggling.

A girl. A happy girl. Without doubt, a girl with pigtails and braces and platform shoes and teardrop glasses and a clear-plastic purse. A Japanese girl born in Ohio, an interpretative dancer, a chemistry major and poet.

"It's Himiko."

"Nope, not me." More giggling. "Yes, yes, it's me. I can't fool you."

When she removed her hands, he caught the smell of something sweet, like green apple lotion, coming from her fingers. It was the same smell that wafted from the poem she slipped under his dorm room door; he associated the scent with her haiku, the one created for his and Takashi's amusement: *They fuck on a dune/two Stealth bombers fly overhead/white sand fills their butts.*

"You stink nice," Nick said.

Himiko stepped in front of him and curtsied.

"Thank you—I think." Then she gave him a quick hug, saying, "So, snob, how come you didn't sit by me?"

"I didn't see you," Nick said.

You have something to tell me, he thought. You always do. What is it?

"You're such a liar, Nick. Anyway—" She motioned for him to lean closer, to bend so she could whisper in his ear: "Tak has a boyfriend, I'm pretty sure. Did you know that? Has he said anything?"

"No."

"No? Guess I'll shut up until he talks to you. Don't want him to think I'm a gossip or anything."

Gratification, melodrama, delight radiated from her. Last year, before becoming Takashi's friend—before being told discreetly that Takashi's romantic feelings weren't for women—she had harbored a massive crush on him, an obsession that at times seemed manic (odd love letters quoting Nine Inch Nails lyrics, an autographed photograph of Morrissey, a feathered bird wing in a plastic baggy—all left for Takashi). But when she finally understood that Takashi was gay and closeted, Himiko became content with his friendship, an alliance of sorts, which Nick found suspect; she had succeeded in getting close to her crush, had offered her confidence and expected his in return. Sharing Takashi's big beanbag chair on those nights when Nick was at the library or in a study group, poring over art books they'd stolen from the campus bookstore (they sometimes scissored pictures and tacked them to the walls), with Camel smoke filling the room, a six-pack of Milwaukee's Best and a bottle of Seagram's Extra Dry Gin on the floor in front of them, they had discussed men and sex and each other's infatuations. She had made herself The Shadow's shadow, felt she knew his private life better than anyone, and enjoyed having the jump on Nick. *Boyfriend*, she said. *Did you know that?* Asking with the same irksome enthusiasm as she said *guess who?*

"Let's get coffee," she said to Nick. "You look like you could use it. You look tired."

"Can't," said Nick. "Got so much reading to do it's insane. Maybe tomorrow though."

She hugged him again, whispering in his ear, "All right, Stranger. Tomorrow." How she loved whispering. How she loved cute things—Happy Meal toys, stuffed animals, cartoon characters—and pleasing tones.

"All right," he whispered, blowing the words into her ear, making her giggle.

And with that, Nick set off, gripping the straps of his backpack, slouching into the evening. He wouldn't run, not now; there was no need. He'd take his time. Yes, he had reading. But that could wait. The air was cool, the birds were still chattering, the grass crunched beneath his sneakers.

He checked his watch. Seventeen past six.

46

7.

A SUITE mate was playing his stereo too loud—stoner music carrying through the bathroom, The Grateful Dead singing, *We can share what we got of yours 'cause we done shared all of mine*—and Nick sat in Takashi's beanbag and tried studying, but he couldn't concentrate to save his life. So instead of focusing on the textbook in his lap, instead of reading about the Andromeda galaxy and its 300 billion stars, he found himself staring at the walls, taking in Takashi's artwork—sketches and paintings hung over the desk, above the bookcase, beside the door. The room was like Takashi's personal gallery, which was fine with Nick because he liked what his roommate created (mostly abstracts done in black and red, geometric shapes twisting around black figures or outlines). But it was Takashi's older stuff that Nick liked best, the stuff painted or drawn before they met: colorful aquarium fish and eels, all crammed together and swimming in different directions; those weren't on the walls anymore, only the newer stuff, and sometimes when Takashi wasn't around Nick dug through his pile of old drawings to find the fishy ones. Then he organized them on the floor, side by side, imagining that he was riding in a glass-bottom boat or standing above a huge aquarium.

Tak, Nick thought, you're going to be famous someday. And then I'll tell everyone how I knew you and how you did your formative work at Moss University, painting and drawing in this little space that we share, our hideout, your studio, my fortified chamber. HQ.

Headquarters, they called their dorm room—or the Brain Trust—where they had their computers (Nick's Compaq laptop, Takashi's Mac on the desk) and a little fridge (stocked with Cokes and Mountain Dew) and a TV (the antennas were broken and the reception lousy) and two portable CD players (both with headphones; that way they could listen to their favorites without bothering each other—The Cure for Takashi, Massive Attack for Nick). They shared a bunk bed, pretending that they were in the army or sleeping underground while the enemy searched for their location. Neither could remember how it was decided, but Takashi got the bottom mattress, Nick the top; it became a joke between them, on account of Takashi being gay: "You're the top," he'd say to Nick, "and I'm the bottom. Let's swap places, take turns."

"I'll pass," Nick would tell him. "I prefer being on top."

But Takashi didn't mean for Nick to know about him being queer. Not that Nick cared. "The way I see it," he told Takashi, "we're all a bit gay, right? Like that bell curve—one end is really faggy, the other end is really unfaggy—and most of us fall somewhere in between those two extremes." And Nick liked the fact that his roommate wasn't effeminate. In fact, in Nick's mind, Takashi was as masculine as they came—had he been a total queen, prancing around their room, dancing to RuPaul or Abba or Pet Shop Boys, getting crazy over Leonardo DiCaprio, wishing he was some character in an Anne Rice book, some creepy vampire—then, Nick figured, he'd have cracked his skull by now. But Takashi wasn't like that, and he and Nick kidded about being twin brothers, born of a Japanese father and an Irish mother, somehow separated at birth. In reality, they had much in common. Both were from West Texas (Nick from Marfa, Takashi from Amarillo), dressed similarly, had skateboards, borrowed each other's clothes. Takashi was The Shadow, because sometimes he just appeared and it was like he was there all along but no one noticed. Nick was Stranger, because he went through a Camus kick and he felt he didn't fit in at Moss—and neither did Takashi. So in a way, Takashi was also Stranger and often Nick was The Shadow. Ying and yang, Nick supposed. Two sides of the same coin. Gay and straight.

Nevertheless, Takashi didn't want his homosexuality established, at least not during his first year at Moss. If Nick hadn't been snooping on the Mac last spring, hoping to find some dirty pictures he suspected Takashi had downloaded, he'd have never known. But the pictures he discovered weren't like anything he expected to find, not by a long shot. No tits, no pussy, no lesbians getting nasty. Just men, lots of them, doing almost everything two or three homosexuals can do together—sucking, fucking, jacking off. Crazy, Nick thought. He probably would've kept the discovery to himself, except there was The Shadow, appearing in the bathroom doorway with a towel around his waist, wet from the shower, catching him. Takashi was angry for days, even though Nick kept saying, "It's totally fine. You're you. It doesn't mean nothing."

"That's not the point, so shut up. I don't want to talk about it."

Fair enough, Nick reasoned.

And after a miserable week of quiet moodiness at HQ, they finally did talk about it. They had coffee at House of Pies and stayed there until dawn. That's when Takashi explained that he considered himself bisexual, although mostly he liked men; he always had, but it took him a long time to deal with it. He'd only slept with one guy, a friend from high school. He told Nick that he never felt stereotypically gay. He didn't like feminine things. He never wanted to be a woman. He always hated Madonna. He said, "All the same, I'd rather ooze out of the closet."

"Whatever's comfortable for you," Nick told him. "It doesn't matter to me."

"I know it doesn't. But it's my business. It's pretty private."

"I guess I'd feel the same way."

"I know you would."

Then everything was okay, to the point where they could even joke about it. Sometimes Takashi made a comment about a good-looking jock he'd see walking by ("God, he's probably dumber than dirt, but I'd blow him in a heartbeat"), and Nick would crack up. Still, Nick had a difficult time imagining Takashi as someone who might like doing that with another guy; it didn't disgust him, but he couldn't picture The Shadow having a lover or a boyfriend. That's what he was thinking as he stared at the art on the walls—Himiko says you've got a boyfriend, and you didn't tell me and I'm kind of hurt. I thought you'd tell me first, Tak. We're twins.

If my words did glow with the gold of sunshine, and my tunes were played on the harp unstrung, would you hear my voice come through the music, would you hold it near as it were your own?

Jerry Garcia was dead, and Nick was grateful. But that didn't stop The Grateful Dead from attacking HQ, from making him want to vomit his dinner. So he retreated. He took his book and left. He escaped down the hallway, where he could still hear the music playing behind him. No big deal. The way he saw it, he was on an important mission. His objective: finding a quiet place to read. Forget that he was exhausted, or that he should be climbing into bed, or that The Shadow was somewhere else, or that The Grateful Dead ever existed—just forget it all as he wandered outside into the night, taking a deep breath, then another, fast. He wondered if he should go back and sleep, but he was already on his way, going forward, heading toward the library, and he couldn't stop himself, so why try.

8.

IT WAS no secret that men once had sex with other men—students with other students—in the library basement at night. But since the doors were removed from the men's restroom stalls and a NO LOITERING placard was mounted above the paper towel dispenser, those nocturnal encounters took place somewhere else; the stadium parking lot was rumored as the new location, so was the quad, with its large trees and unlighted sidewalks. Regardless, Nick was glad the activity had left the basement; otherwise he wouldn't be studying there now. Nor would he feel comfortable using the restroom, the entrance of which he could spy from where he sat—when someone wandered in, that person soon wandered out, alone.

In the quiet surrounding him, Nick could read for hours, chew his pen cap, yawn, and rest his eyes without bother. Often he slept, but it was never his intention to do so. Something about the silence, about sitting with his homework, among the reference stacks, off at the table he thought of as belonging only to him; it was easy to fall asleep, to fold hands over the open textbook, fingers for a pillow. One moment he'd be contemplating the universe or a poem, the next moment—

An ambiguous slumber (shaped by the hiss and glow of long fluorescent bulbs), offering dreams he couldn't recall. Perhaps he went elsewhere in his basement sleep, returning to his West Texas high school in Marfa (sprinting around the track field, or doing laps in the gym), maybe riding his bicycle near his childhood home in Arizona (peddling along that dirt road between Mexico and his stepfather's farm). He was never sure. And when he stirred—aware of the spit on his chin, the pages crumpling under his hands—his body usually felt heavier, his muscles stiff, as if he'd extracted himself from someplace confining and finite and distant.

He thought: What's happening? Where'd I go?

But not tonight. Not yet. Because only now was he resting his right cheek against his hands. For a bit his eyes remained unclosed, a vertical stare, taking in his part of the library—the bookshelves that concealed him, the aisle leading directly to the water fountain and men's restroom. How odd it seemed to Nick, in those seconds before drifting away, that the basement bathroom didn't have doors on the stalls. How funny that was; all those pent-up, horny Moss students from years past, cruising among the stacks, meeting in the restroom, screwing. Bad enough for the university to take notice. Bad enough for doors to get carted.

He smiled, closing his eyes. The overhead bulbs hummed. He sensed the ultraviolet light flickering, the cathode weakening, until—already dreaming—his lips parted.

Fingers snap snap snapping.

"I command you to wake. You're not a chicken anymore, you're Nick again. You're no long under my influence."

There was Takashi, leaning over the table, hovering at Nick's ear. And there was Nick, stirring, eyes blinking open, his pillow hands wet with drool.

"Wake up, zonked boy."

"I am."

Nick raised his head, wiping his hands on his jeans, and watched as Takashi settled into the seat beside him, placing an oversized art book between them—*Franz Kline: Art and the Structure of Identity*.

"Where'd you come from?" Nick asked.

Takashi grinned mysteriously.

"If I told you I'd have to kill you."

"Then kill me."

"Not a chance."

Not a chance. The Shadow smelled of Polo cologne,

and his black hair—a far cry from the mess that usually peeked from beneath his Fubu baseball cap—was gelled and styled, making Nick think of a high schooler embarking on his first date: hair meticulously combed, the cologne dabbed on the neck and behind the ears, the condom kept ready in the wallet but never used.

Please mention your boyfriend, Tak, so I don't have to ask.

"I need caffeine," Nick said, yawning. Then he added, "Caffeine and good conversation."

"You need sleep."

"No, I need coffee. You need some too. House of Pies?"

"I'll pass, thanks," said Takashi. "I got some work to do, you know, cramming for that Psych quiz."

"You'll go blind cramming."

"Whatever."

Then, for an instant, their eyes locked—brown irises fixed on blue irises—and they said nothing. And it seemed to Nick that Takashi had something to disclose, something important to reveal. Instead, he said, "Hey, you get my note about the meeting?"

Nick nodded.

"Yeah, I was late—but I didn't miss much. You didn't either." Then he explained about the meeting the following week (the voting on pieheads, the Chief Creamers wanting creative targets). He mentioned seeing Himiko, and, surprising himself with abruptness in which the words came, blurted, "You got a boyfriend, she told me, she wondered if I knew."

"Don't have a boyfriend," said Takashi with a tight smile.

"Didn't think you did. Unless you were keeping a secret or something."

Was it relief Nick suddenly felt? Or guilt at having been so tactless? He wasn't sure, even as Takashi said, "No secrets between me and you, I promise. But Himiko, I swear, she's so nosy. She thinks I got a boyfriend because I act like I do and I won't tell her anything. You'd be the first to know anyway."

"I don't really care," Nick lied. "It's your life."

Takashi reached for the art book, flipping it open.

"Actually, this is my life—"

As he began turning the pages—leisurely, pausing a long moment on each Kline print (all those harsh black lines against white, like Japanese calligraphy gone wrong)—Nick scrutinized him, the profile of his face and the softness of his skin, an attractive, unblemished, Asian complexion; Nick understood the careful turning of the pages as reverent and considerate, and he knew that soon Takashi would stop on a print that caught his interest and caress it with his fingers. It was inevitable, and it was contagious: Takashi had been the one who dragged him to the Menil Collection, that free museum near the gay bars on Montrose, where—if the hands were quicker than the security guards' glances— fingertips could quickly stroke a Warhol soup can, a Pollock dripping, a Magritte bowler hat, a Kline brushstroke (each having been touched by The Shadow and Stranger). But Franz Kline, crony of de Kooning and Pollock, was the agreed-upon favorite. Nick and Takashi spent hours studying the man's large canvases, pressing their fingertips against the white and black oils, sometimes doing homework on the benches placed in front of his bigger pieces. There was a particular painting—done in black oils, a dark landscape obscured by a darker rain, a requiem for Hiroshima—which Takashi returned to time and time again, keeping a cautious distance. That huge painting, reminding him of his great uncle Dr. Shimura, who, having survived the August 1945 bombing of Hiroshima, tended patients at the A-Bomb Hospital, until leukemia finally claimed him. That single painting, he had no desire to touch it.

Now, in the library basement with Nick beside him, Takashi's fingers started moving, gently rubbing a print entitled *The Bridge*; he couldn't help himself, even though the print lacked texture or bumps—just smooth paper that was curiously cold. Then, as Nick stifled a yawn, Takashi flattened his palm on the page—and they locked eyes again and began laughing at Takashi's foolishness.

9.

Nick's '78 Chevy was older than he by two years, but the old truck ran well. Never mind that the tinted windshield was cracked from one side to the other, or that the muffler sputtered like a tommy gun, or that the tape player delighted in eating his cassettes. At least the interior was in decent shape; his stepfather had the seats re-upholstered, got the engine tuned and hoses changed, before handing Nick the keys on the eve of high school graduation: "She'll get you where you're going, son. She'll get you to Houston and back home for Christmas break."

Except home wasn't in West Texas anymore. Not after his stepfather quit his job as a roughneck. Not after his mom and stepfather moved to Durango, Colorado, where they operated their own pizza parlor—The Pig Slice. But, Nick reasoned, that was how it'd always been—the farm in Arizona, the drilling crew in Texas, the restaurant in Colorado. They'll probably end up in Utah by the time I get out of college, he thought. They'll probably be selling foot-long hot dogs in Wyoming.

"Nope, we're staying put," his mom assured him. "Believe me, there's good money in pizza. It's almost as nice as hitting oil."

When Nick talked to them on the phone, his parents sounded happy. His mom said she couldn't wait for him to see their new pre-fab home, his stepfather raved about the fishing; they both promised that Nick would love their special pizza crust, which was made with beer and garlic. But Nick wouldn't be going anywhere for Christmas. Durango was a long way away, and he felt certain the truck wouldn't get him there. Furthermore, Colorado sounded too cold in December (his mom mentioned an awful story about a pair of teenage hikers getting lost in a blizzard and freezing to death), while the relative warmth of Houston was more pleasant. And, truth be known, he didn't really have a desire to travel anywhere else.

Still, as far as distant places went, Nick sometimes missed the desolation around Marfa. While in high school there, he couldn't wait to leave. He hated the town and the people (all those provincials who ragged him because he didn't play football, because he had a skateboard), hated his stepfather coming home dirty and tired and mean from work, hated his mom bending over backwards catering to the man—doing his laundry, cooking what he liked, cleaning the gunk from underneath his fingernails. But mostly Nick missed just being in the country, removed from everything, and watching the stars by himself. Nevertheless, it was his stepfather who first showed him the constellations, who bought him a telescope when he was thirteen and told him where to look. And since his stepfather stopped drinking, he'd been a decent kind of guy; of course, seeing how Nick never knew his biological father, there was no one to compare the man to. "I can't say our relationship is close or anything," he told Takashi, "more like a coach and a player, but he's okay. I mean, he took me camping, helped with my homework, didn't get pissed when I got my nose pierced—and he gave me that truck, just slapped the keys in my palm, saying, 'Tank is full. She's yours, take her.'"

Take her he did. Zooming right out of West Texas and down to the Gulf, heading toward Moss University like an escapee from Hicksville Prison. In his first year or so in Houston, she never failed him once, never fell apart or stopped running. Yet each excursion—whether it was to the grocery store, or a day on Galveston Island with Takashi, or a cruise along I-10—felt like it might be the last. Sometimes Nick thought she might expire while chugging up to a red light, her noisy muffler telling him, "I'm getting too old for this, don't know how much longer I got." But that's what

57

made driving the Chevy an adventure; every trip, every little jaunt, had him wondering if he'd reach his destination.

And tonight, while pulling into a space in front of House of Pies, he knew an old truck was better than no truck. Even an old truck that crept along, that created a racket as it idled, that continued groaning for a bit after the engine was turned off. Walking into the diner, he was grateful for two things— his Chevy kept running, House of Pies was open all night. *House of Guys*, that's what Takashi called it, because when the clubs let out the place grew packed with a mixed bag of characters (drunk jocks, drag queens, gay couples, earnest students with notebooks and backpacks), all crowding the booths and drinking coffee and smoking.

Clutching his astronomy textbook, Nick did a beeline for the diner's dessert display case, where he then stood and contemplated those amazing pies, practically slobbering at the sight of his favorites. Chocolate Chiffon. Grasshopper. Sour Cream and Raisin Cream. Orange Meringue. French Silk. Double-Crust Nectarine. Fudge Ribbon. Works of art encircled by a beautifully finished pastry edge, rivaled only by his mom's Crumb-Topped Gooseberry. If the Crusters had any class, he thought, these would be the pies we'd use (high-tech weapons in the pie assassination game, as opposed to the simple whipped cream numbers the pieheads get nailed with). But the House of Pies' desserts were too expensive, and too good for wasting on most targets; he'd rather humiliate himself with the French Silk than let the pieheads savor the chocolate and vanilla dripping down their faces.

"Sexy treats," a voice behind him whispered. "Yum yum."

Nick spotted Himiko's reflection in the glass, peering over him, and he expected her to start hassling him for being at the diner. *Thought you had too much reading to do, thought you couldn't get coffee tonight.* But instead she rested her chin on his shoulder and sighed through her nose, expelling congested air from her nostrils.

"Tasty yum munch."

If you say something like that again, Nick wanted to say, I'll slap you unconscious and squish you dead. Suddenly he found himself imagining what she'd look like with Black-Bottom Pie smeared across her face—forehead, hair, and cheeks all brown and gummy, covered in a gluey mask smelling of rum.

"Yummers snack snack."

Then Himiko slipped her arms around his rib cage and, gaping at the pies, began squeezing his sides, massaging him with a gentle pressure from her fingers, until she worked her fingers up his spine, put both small hands on his shoulders, and the two of them stared at their reflections in the glass—where a transparent smirk and frown floated over a yellow meringue topping.

HIMIKO

10.

LAST MAY, a week before the end of their freshman year, Himiko had asked Takashi, "What exactly is a Lai Lai," and Takashi replied, "Sorry, what was that?" She sighed for effect, rolling her eyes; he hadn't heard a word she'd spoken, was too preoccupied with whatever Nick was saying.

Nearby, a waitress and a waiter were arguing in Cantonese, something about a miscalculated takeout order ticket.

Himiko said, "It's Lai Lai Dumpling House, right? Except I've never seen a Lai Lai on the menu. So what is it?"

Takashi said, "I don't know, maybe a province or something."

They were sitting at a table beside the front door, where close by an elderly Chinese couple and a Hispanic family stood, all crowded into the small restaurant and hoping for the next available seats. It was Nick's nineteenth birthday, and Takashi and Himiko had decided to bring him to a favorite dive in the Asian suburbs (the servings were large, the prices cheap). The meals offered at Lai Lai Dumpling House were worthy of any celebration; the owner and majordomo—derisively called "Madam Woo" by Himiko—was always quick to mention that the pork steamed dumplings were unrivaled in Houston: "I know," Himiko had told her. "That's why we're here." And Nick was now gazing at Madame Woo, watching as she approached the waiting patrons, flashing a put-on smile, saying, "Hello, just a few minutes more please, okay?" Or rather he was studying her—the tight red formal dress her plump body had managed to occupy, the enormous and styled black hair that dwarfed her head.

Himiko said, "Nick, you'll go blind."

Takashi said, "He's already going blind, but not because of her," then he placed a hand on Nick's shoulder, leaving it there.

Nick laughed. He patted Takashi's hand, seemingly comfortable with where it rested.

Himiko had never seen the two so intimate. Perhaps Nick was just tolerating Takashi's affection, she imagined, because he was getting a free dinner. Or perhaps it was something else. Then after Nick had excused himself to use the restroom, she nudged Takashi with an elbow, whispering, "Hey, do you think he's gay? I mean, he's never had a girlfriend, isn't very interested in women, true? Or is he?"

"To be honest, I haven't a clue. It hasn't come up."

She cocked an eyebrow.

"You know, Tak, I bet he's a virgin, so he doesn't know. A gay virgin is more like it, don't you think?"

Takashi reached for his Coke, saying nothing.

She nudged him again and blew in his ear and then said, "Don't you think about it at all? Don't you like him?"

He said, "Sure, I've thought about it—and yes—I like him. But I don't think he is, so it's something I'd prefer not to get hung up on."

She said, "Maybe you should."

"Why do you care?" But he didn't let her answer: "I need to piss." Then he was out of his seat and heading toward the restroom—and Himiko sat there staring at the remnants of their dinner (half a serving tray of triple meat flat fried rice noodles, a steamer with three tepid pork dumplings), wondering what Nick and Takashi were talking about in the restroom.

Like a couple of girls, she thought. Like a couple of women.

BING

11.

ORIGINS OF the Universe was floundering, and Bing couldn't have been more pleased. How many students had dropped the class last week? Almost twenty by his count. How many this week? Sixteen, maybe seventeen. And where was White Girl Disease? He hadn't heard a peep from her. Perhaps you haven't dropped, he thought. Perhaps aliens abducted you. Perhaps your lifeless body has been thrown into space and is now drifting toward the sun.

"That girl is a waste of molecules," he told Damien. "All of them are, all of the undergrads, excluding maybe one or two. But I don't care. If each child quits, then I'm a happier man. I'll be free from that disgraceful course."

They were sitting in front of Eric's Rotisserie, sipping white zinfandel at an outside table, enjoying a bright fall afternoon (much warmer weather than was expected for September).

"Know what I think," Damien said, holding his wine glass near his chin, "I think you hate women."

"That's ridiculous," Bing replied, his sudden irritation bubbling to the surface. "What a stupid comment. I like women fine."

"I think you're threatened by them."

"What nonsense."

"Really—?"

"What would you know about me and women? What do you know about women anyway?" Never before had Bing felt so utterly annoyed at Damien. "You probably hate them more than anyone I know."

"Look, I call it how I see it, but—" Damien paused as though weighing his words, then he quickly added, "It's only my opinion."

"Well, it's baseless," Bing said uneasily. "I love women, just not stupid women. Unfortunately, I encounter so few smart ones."

If his day, up until that moment, hadn't gone smoothly—if Bing had had to deal with any of the Trinity, or had allowed himself to feel deserted by his students—he would've grabbed his briefcase, gulped his wine in a flash, and then left Damien without saying goodbye. But it was a wonderful afternoon, crisp and warm at the same time, accentuating Bing's already high spirits (the zinfandel didn't hurt either). He refused to let his mood darken. When considering his conversation with Nick after class—how the boy had smiled at him, how they'd walked leisurely together across the quad en route to Bing's office—there wasn't a single aspersion Damien might cast that was worth being irritated about.

"Everyone has opinions about their friends, I suppose. It's better leaving some things unsaid, right?"

He wanted Damien to be aware of Nick (though he decided against mentioning their meeting now), of how the boy had stood before Bing's desk—listening with long arms dangling at his sides, thoughtful blue eyes blinking, as Bing offered his proposal—of how Nick carried a fragrance that filled the office; underarm deodorant, giving off a some-what minty aroma.

An independent study then?

"Sure," Nick had said repeatedly, "that'd be great."

Because the boy was obviously more intelligent and more serious than his peers. An independent study that convened once a week—say, at Bing's house on Friday mornings, from eight to noon—replacing any attendance required for the Tuesday/Thursday classes?

"Sure."

Pure discussion. No tests, no final.

"Sounds awesome."

Not Origins of the Universe (yet the grade would corre-

spond to that course on the transcript), but bigger issues—
the possibility of vacuum-bubble formation, inflationary
theory, black holes containing the end of time.

"That'd be great."

So Bing wrote down his home phone number and
address, handing it to Nick with a wink.

"There you go."

"Great."

They shook hands.

"See you Friday, Nick."

"Sure, I look forward to it. Thanks."

Mission accomplished, as simple as that.

Leaves had fallen from trees and were lying in a bunch
several feet from the table; a reminder of summer's end,
curled and withered on the ground, waiting to be swept
away.

"We need another round," Bing grumbled as he finished
his glass.

At nearby tables, plates with bits of food and empty beer
bottles remained uncollected and flies were buzzing around
them.

"Where's that waiter? He's not very good."

"You know, I don't hate women," Damien said, grinning, lifting his wine glass so that sunlight could shine
through it. "I just like men more."

But Bing ignored him. He turned his glass upside-down
on the table and looked away, at the fallen leaves.

12.

IN BING'S upstairs study, morning light illuminated the windows. On the lawn below, the sun had begun filtering through the elms, touching the grass and warming Susan's bed of wilting perennials; at least another two hours would pass until its rays angled into the study, hitting the carpet where Bing now stood (gazing from the window, coffee mug in hand). Downstairs in the kitchen, Susan was washing clean the breakfast plates. He could hear her talking to herself, her mumbling mixed with the sound of running water. Soon she would be wiping the countertop, continually spraying a sponge with Formula 409, preparing a sanitary surface on which to make egg-salad sandwiches for lunch—before retiring to her bedroom, at nine, so she could watch television.

He tested the coffee with his tongue, still too hot, and thought of how, during breakfast, he'd given his wife thirty dollars (a considerably larger donation for her charities than usually expected): "A student is visiting this morning. If you'd put something together for lunch—just leave it in the fridge for us—I'd appreciate it." He'd had to bribe her. Understanding overtook the confusion on her face, and she nodded dutifully while pocketing the cash.

"Sandwiches," she'd said, "and chips."

Bing turned from the window and went to sit on the couch. As he began nursing the mug he watched Pussy play on the throw rug near the doorway, chasing her tail in a circle like a dog. For a moment he wondered—had Nick forgotten or perhaps overslept, as college students sometimes do? Had he lost the address of the house? Of course not. So what was taking him so long? It was already after eight. Still in the shower? Getting dressed? There was no way to know. But Nick, at nineteen, had seemed responsible enough—he'd never missed class (even on those days when Bing was tardy), always took notes (even when Bing had little to say). The boy appeared so inward and studious (one could have called him somber) that he seemed completely unaware of how beautiful he was.

So where are you?

Pussy bit lazily at her tail, spun half-heartedly a final time, no longer interested in the chase. Then she plopped on her side, stretching her paws out, and closed her eyes.

"Always something!" his wife yelled.

Her voice reached the study, clearly audible for only a moment: Susan was shouting at no one, carrying on as she scrubbed the counter; she couldn't help herself, the things she said, the way they often erupted from her. But Bing listened anyway, knowing she'd stop forthwith.

"Always something, always something!"

Then silence.

He set the mug on the coffee table, trading it for a hard-back copy of his book—*Exploding Stars: Complexity And Destruction Examined*—which he'd taken from a box in his bedroom closet (a box sent from his publisher, filled with first edition printings of the volume). He glanced to his right, holding the hardback out. "This is for you," he said, pretending Nick was sitting beside him on the couch. "My book."

He imagined the boy's face brightening. His thin, delicate lips parting with surprise.

"You don't own it, do you?" he'd ask.

Then Bing would remove the pen from his breast pocket.

"Here—I'll sign it, if you'd like—so you won't forget who gave it to you."

He'd open the book on his lap, turning to the title page, and write: *For Nick—With great admiration for his mind— anticipation for knowing him and his ideas—and confidence in our friendship.* The boy would be pleased, delighted, of course, at such a fond sentiment. Perhaps slightly embarrassed. As if Professor Owen had said too much.

But Bing would behave less like a friend today and more like a lecturer. Before sharing the confidence of friendship, he'd get to know Nick better (how many Fridays did the semester have?).

"There you go. Enjoy, okay? Just do me a favor from now on—don't ever be late again, right? Our time together is important. You have a lot to learn."

A vehicle rattled into the driveway, sputtering and growling, quieting abruptly. Was it the engine that created such horrendous noise? The muffler? Sunlight reflected off something from below—a side mirror or the windshield—casting a bright circle against the ceiling of the study. Bing crossed to the window and stared down. He spotted Nick, climbing from his clunker of a truck, fresh faced, backpack hanging on a shoulder, chewing gum, the slender picture of health. "You're here," he said to himself, smoothing his hair with a hand. And added with displeasure, "I've been waiting for you."

13.

THESE ARE some of the things Nick touched—a pen, a fork, a plate, a glass, a book, the bathroom doorknob, the toilet handle, the hand towel beside the sink, Pussy the cat. And these were the things that—once Nick had said goodbye for the day, once the boy had started his clamorous truck—Bing found himself drawn to (most of which sat on his coffee table). The routine was always the same: From the glass Nick had used, he drank what was left. He licked the end of the fork. He nibbled whatever crumbs remained on the boy's plate, often compelled to chew a half-eaten sandwich or a potato chip. Then in the bathroom, Bing smelled the damp hand towel, jiggled the toilet handle, stood before the bowl (trying hard to envision Nick standing in the exact position, pants unzipped, legs apart while he urinated) and masturbated.

Afterwards, in his study, he gathered Pussy, cradling her in his arms, stroking her head as she purred, and lounged lengthwise across the couch.

"Daddy loves his baby, yes he does."

Then did he nap?

He was never certain, perhaps just resting his eyes.

As the weather grew cooler, as Nick's clothing became thicker—sweaters and jackets and long-sleeved shirts—Bing would relax after their meetings with a quilt pulled over his body, Pussy sleeping on his chest.

And in those moments did he recall what he and Nick had talked about? Did he ponder their discussions?

Sometimes.

September: Gravitational radiation and formation of black holes. High-energy particle physics and the big bang. Collapsing-cosmos paradox and gravity. Proton decay and neutrinos. Nick and his future ("Don't know yet. I've thought about English as a major, maybe teaching—I'd like to write."). Nick and his family ("My father died when I was little—and my mother remarried when I was nine— then we moved around some—"). Nick and his love life ("A girlfriend? Nah. Haven't really had the time, or interest, I guess. Maybe later. It's not a big deal.").

"Are the sandwiches okay?"

"Yeah, they're great. Pretty tasty."

"If you'd like something else next week—something more substantial—let me know. Susan is a wonderful cook. She really is."

"That's cool, but sandwiches are fine."

"Would you like some wine, perhaps? I have beer as well."

"That's okay. I don't really drink—thanks though."

"Mind if I do?"

"No, not at all. Go ahead."

October: Fusion energy and eventual explosion of stars. Bubble formation and baby universes and vacuum states. Mathematical model of decay in false-vacuum states. Thermodynamic equilibrium in the universe. Life at Moss University and Nick ("It's okay, I guess, but everyone seems so uptight—it's hard to explain—just like everyone's in a hurry to get somewhere, but no one's sure why they're here or where they're going"). Girls and Nick ("Thanks, but I don't think I'm all that good-looking or whatever. As far as girls go, I can take them or leave them. It's not like they come banging on my door or anything"). Nick and Bing ("I don't know, it's kind of weird not calling you Professor Owen, Bing. Give me some time to get used to it. I might slip up every now and then and call you professor").

"Some wine, Nick?"

"Maybe a little. Sure."

"I have beer too."

"Wine is fine. I hate the taste of beer, makes my mouth feel all cottony."

"Well, I think you'll like this. It's not too dry, has a sweet aftertaste."

"Sounds good—"

"Really, there's nothing like wine shared between friends. You know, let's have a toast to that—what do you say? To friendship—"

November.

Bing made the calculations. He'd paid his wife a total of two hundred and ten dollars in the last seven weeks, such hefty compensation for smearing egg salad between bread. And with Thanksgiving approaching—how much would he have to pay for thawing the turkey, for preparing the meal? Especially since he'd already invited Nick. Perhaps he'd appeal to her sense of charity: "The boy's family is in Colorado. He's stuck here and I'm sure he'd love a home cooked meal." But he'd also invited Casey, that rogue colleague deprived of family in Texas, who, as long as Tong was still on sabbatical, remained Bing's one true ally in the department. "These are my friends," he'd tell her. "These are the only people who care for me and what I do, Susan. So I'll leave a blank check on the stove—but please don't disappoint me."

Now, while resting on the couch with Pussy, he knew she'd acquiesce. She'd understand. Even if it meant giving her carte blanche. She wouldn't let him down. Even if he had to scare her—if he had to say, "I think I might be ill." He wouldn't mention masturbating in front of the toilet, wouldn't go into detail about the sudden appearance of blood in his semen—how today the viscous mess landed in the bowl, red woven into white, swirling around as the toilet flushed. He'd just tell her, "I'm afraid there's something terribly wrong with me, dear, so I suspect I'll be seeing an internist," and, without question, she'd remove the turkey from the freezer.

TONG

14.

THE STARS are threshed, and the souls are threshed from their husks.
Was it Yeats who wrote that line? Or Blake? Tong couldn't recall. Still, he wanted his supernova to have a name of importance, a title that suggested romance and beauty: Yeats' Neutron Star, possibly Blake's Luminosity. Unfortunately, someone else had named his discovery, logging it as SN 1999B. But Tong didn't mind all that much, it was his supernova regardless. And in the months following the star's explosion, he had dutifully recorded every bit of collected data, preparing detailed notes for the paper he'd soon write. In his cramped work space at McDonald Observatory—wire-rimmed bifocals perched on his nose, fingertips pressed to his bald scalp—Tong poured over his findings, occasionally adding lengthy interpretations on a yellow legal pad (so much to delineate, the minutiae could be painstaking). But how dry it all was, how incredibly flat—and where was the majesty, the poetics concerning what had been, after all, a fantastic occurrence?

If he could gaze inside a star the very second all fusion ceased, Tong knew that layers of different elements would be seen (iron forming the core with the lighter elements around the wider radii). In small mass stars, the less heavy elements furthest from the core burned poorly while the material near the surface enkindled fleetingly, releasing a tiny amount of energy. But in a tremendous supernova such as SN 1999B, the heat beyond the core would be insignificant enough to allow proper fusion in the subsequent layers. So as fusion started beyond the core, persisting for a short time, the star would still be doomed—the subsequent compacting gravitational power executing a violent death of marvelous speed and intensity; in seconds the core would collapse, yet the consequent destruction would proceed at a slower rate than that of the imploding iron center. As a result, the star's surface would exist for quite a while unscathed, wholly oblivious to the onslaught erupting within—until, at last, the havoc burst through the outer layers, ripping the exterior apart.

So Tong would embellish the event. He would protract the drama, adding words like "dissolution" and "quietus" and "iridescence," for there was lyricism and richness in supernovae, especially in his—not just mere facts. Of course, he felt certain, many of his colleagues would naturally debate his characterization of his star's final moments, as Bing had already done in a recent e-mail: *Nothing fancy or quasi-poetic about it. The cosmos simply operated in accord with physical laws. An unadorned and more scientific description of the physical factors involved in SN 1999B's demise should give a clear enough account of the universe at work. No descriptive subtleties or slight personification need apply. Good God, man, I'm rambling. Ever get the feeling your insides are going bad and your outside hasn't a clue? Ha! Give me a call when you get a chance, I'd love to talk with you. My world isn't the same without you around, my friend. I understand there are snakes in West Texas. There are snakes in Houston too.*

NICK

15.

LIN BIAO was the son of Chinese immigrants, a Chemical Engineering student, and an outspoken evangelical Christian. At Moss he went by his Anglo surname, a moniker decided upon after lengthy consideration and prayer—Norman (Norm or Normy to those who knew him well). Though among the Crusters he was regarded as University Enemy #1, an obvious piehead begging for a creamy splatter. In the recent past, the group had tolerated Norman's long-winded editorial rants in the school newspaper. Last month he'd denounced Halloween as *a glorification of Satan's influence on American culture that is a mockery of everything sacred and holy, even stooping low enough to make innocent children dress like witches and other bidders of the Dark One's will*; the month before he'd referred to the annual Night of Decadence—that late night drunken blowout in which students wore as little clothing as possible—as *a complete degradation of the human soul and being, an excuse for shameless drinking and casual sex, tolerated by a God-less institution that purports to exist for the enriching of our minds, but has lost its obligation to the Higher Source somewhere along the way*!

But this month Norman went too far; with the Screw Your Roommate Dance approaching on the student agenda, he wrote: *The very notion that S***w Your Roommate is not seen for the abomination that it is sickens me to no end. The 'tradition' of setting up your roommate with a blind date for the sole purpose of sex is not only disgusting but vile in the face of all that is decent. It is an offensive and disturbing copulation. Where and why have things gone so wrong? More people should be upset by this 'tradition' that treats sex like a piece of candy rather than what it was intended* *for—the expression of God's love shared between a married man and woman, resulting in children who are pure and wanted. You might not like what I'm about to say, but those who partake in S***w Your Roommate next week are fools for not seeing that they are shaming themselves and those they have to live with. Am I the only one who feels ashamed that he is a student at Moss? Am I the only one who will speak out about this evil tradition?*

Norman had missed the point. Yes, blind dates were arranged. Yes, some students had sex with their surprise escorts. But the general idea behind the dance was a humorous screw—the participants weren't usually that interested in one another to begin with (though on occasion friendships and unrequited crushes blossomed into romance). Last year, Nick had set Takashi up with Himiko—and, aided by Himiko's mischievous roommate, Takashi had done the same for Nick. So the threesome attended the event together, dancing side by side for a while, eventually opting to people watch while drinking fruit punch in a corner. Their evening concluded on a dormitory roof, where—engaging in an activity far removed from offensive and disturbing copulation—they attempted to spot Polaris with binoculars.

Of course, Norman had written, *the organizers of this dance, if you can call it that, are attempting to subvert the moral foundation of the student body. What shall be next? A keg party in which crosses and Bibles are burned for fun? One can't help but wonder and worry. At this point, nothing the campus ringleaders of depravity could sanction would amaze me. Sadly, Moss is on a slippery slope indeed.*

That was the final straw. Bill and Debra, the Chief Creamers, had had enough of Mr. Biao's opinions (principally because they were on the planning committee for Screw Your Roommate and felt slighted by his editorial comments), and so the Pi Crusters assembled for a secret emergency meeting.

"You know, you cut the Christians slack," Debra told the others, "you try to ignore them, and then some asshole just can't keep his self-righteous mouth shut—so what do you do?"

"He's done crossed the line," Bill concurred, affecting his good ol' boy persona. "He's gonna be in a heap of stickiness by week's end."

How easy it was luring University Enemy #1 to the ambush. A single e-mail did the trick, sent under a pseudonym by Nick and Takashi: *Norman, I was very impressed by your words in the newspaper. As a student here at Moss I too have been disgusted by The S***w Your Roommate Dance. I just wish there was some sort of alternative gathering on the same night so those of us with the same feelings could meet and have fun with other like-minded Christians. Would you consider helping me to organize such an event, or in the very least discuss ideas and options? Please let me know. Look forward to hearing from you. Yours truly—Monica Chow.*

His reply came in less than an hour.

Monica, thanks for your kind remarks about my editorials. As you can imagine, a lot of people aren't happy about what I say, but as long as I can take a position for what is right then I'm willing to continue writing the Truth. Anyway, I too have been thinking of an alternative to S***w Your Roommate, and would love the opportunity to put something together. I know Campus Crusade for Christ would gladly sponsor whatever event we can organize. Maybe we can meet at the library tomorrow. I'm free in the afternoon. How about at 3? Let me know.

Monica: *Tomorrow at 3 is perfect. I'll meet you in front of the library. I'll be wearing a red sweater and my hair is very very short and black. :-) If I'm not there at exactly 3 don't worry, I'll be there soon. Hope to see you then. I'm sure I'll recognize you from your picture in the paper.*

He was hard to miss, loitering on the library steps,

hands in his pockets, round eyeglasses glinting every time he turned his head and gazed at a female student walking past. Are you Monica? How about you? Perhaps you? Monica?

The Crusters attacked at 3:05—some coming from within the library, others stepping out from behind the wide pillars near the entrance, while others moved quickly up the steps—all zeroing in on their target, who seemed, for a moment, oblivious to what was about to happen. But as the first pie was flung—followed rapidly by the second, third, and fourth—he crouched, shielding his face with his hands.

Six more pies hit him.

Norman jerked backward against a pillar and buckled to his knees.

Three more pies.

"No," he said. His hair was matted with whipped cream.

Two more pies.

Then almost as soon as they came forward the Crusters retreated, dispersing in different directions, leaving University Enemy #1 to be laughed at by onlookers. In the golden light his spattered head and chest were more yellow than white. He appeared to be melting, a strange snowman disintegrating on a warm afternoon.

"What's funny—?"

Norman slumped on the steps, straightening his back against the pillar. Cream dripped down his lips, and he sighed, deeply.

"You bastards," he finally said, lifting his stained glasses and glaring at the bystanders. "Stupid bastards!"

Three days later, his editorial concluded with, *Like my parents suffering from the suppression of their religious beliefs and their freedom of speech in China, I too have been persecuted for what I believe. How can such things happen at a university? Isn't this where we are supposed to learn and to teach? Then why is it that someone whose opinion isn't the same as others has to go through what I went through? How much longer before the quad turns into Tiananmen Square? I wonder. As for The Pi Crusters, it is not for me to judge any of you. All I can do is take solace in the fact that God has His own pies waiting for each and every one of you to taste—and His pies aren't as sweet as you might think.*

16.

AT HIS library basement table, Nick shut Bing's book and leaned back in his chair, gazing at the white empty wall across the room. He tried pretending that Himiko wasn't sitting beside him (she'd appeared moments earlier, landing in the seat without speaking, biting her nails while Nick studied), and instead considered the passage he'd just read, the troubling words hard to forget: *Regarding the world of microphysics, it is very possible that we exist in a metastable universe. Unexpectedly, a bubble of true vacuum could form a nucleus in space, ballooning to an astronomical size, growing outwards at the speed of light, destroying everything in its path—including, of course, us. In fact, this kind of universe-destroying bubble could possibly (and no doubt accidentally) be set off by particle physicists using the next generation of particle accelerators. It's hardly difficult to imagine an extremely high-energy collision of subatomic particles bringing about such conditions in which—beginning here on earth, in less than a nanosecond, erupting from a small area of land—our universe could simply vanish.*

Nick shuddered, uncertain if the goosepimples rising underneath his shirt had anything to do with sudden universal annihilation, or, as he suspected, were the result of the basement air being so frigid. Both, he concluded.

"I know a secret," Himiko said.

He rocked forward in his chair, cupping his face in his hands, avoiding her stare. Mumbling through his fingers, he said, "Do I care? Let me see—uh, no, I don't."

"Well, it's only a little secret concerning you and a Screw Your Roommate date Tak has found for you."

He moved a hand, peeking at her, an eyeball showing between a thumb and forefinger.

"Who?"

"I'm not saying, so there."

Nick lowered his hands to the desk, shrugging.

"That's fine. As long as it's not you then I don't mind."

"And what's wrong with me?" asked Himiko softly, folding her arms at her chest.

"Nothing—except it's a new year and I expect a new date, that's all."

She frowned, pouting her lips.

"You're mean. Don't you think I'm beautiful, Nick? I think I'm beautiful."

You are, he wanted to say. In a goofy kind of way.

"Are you going to tell me, Himiko?"

"No."

"How come?"

"Because it's a secret."

Nick nodded. Then he fluttered a hand at her, as if to sweep her away.

"Scram," he said.

Her pout shifted into a sly grin: "All right, I might tell you if you tell me who you've found for Tak."

"Whatever. It doesn't matter." He didn't seem to relish the idea as much as she did. "If you really want to know, I haven't found anyone yet. I don't even know who to ask."

"I do," she said. "Can I help you set him up?"

"I guess, if you want—"

"Because I know someone who really likes him."

"Who is it?"

She began gathering his things, organizing them into a neat stack.

"Better come with me."

"Where?"

"Don't ask questions. You want my help or not?"

Nick said nothing, watching passively as she took his notebook, his pen, Bing's book—slipping them all inside his open backpack.

"Then come on—it won't take long, I promise."

She was right, it took less than five minutes. Up the stairs they went, Himiko leading, wandering past the Computer Lab, into the lobby, heading toward the checkout counter. And there he was—green hair, pierced eyebrow, pale skinny arms, scanning books behind the counter and then setting them on a cart marked To Be Shelved: Warren Nathan, a Library Science major and, in Nick's opinion, a snotty dullard ("Whitman's incredibly overrated," he recalled Warren once saying in an English seminar. "As for great American poets, I much prefer the texture and insight of Ginsberg, the esoterica of Plath").

"Hey, Himiko, what's going on, girl?"

"Nothing much. But we wanted to ask you something."

Nick, turning around so that his back faced Warren, stifled a sigh. And as Himiko and Warren talked, their conversation now hushed and serious, they paid him no attention. Students moved by as if trudging in snow drifts, the warmth of summer lingering faintly in their memories. But Nick's mind was elsewhere, floating somewhere in space like a lost satellite, and while he conjured subatomic particles colliding and erupting and ballooning, his body was chilled to the bone.

"God, I'd love to go out with him. He's gorgeous."

"I know," Himiko said, giggling. "Then you're his date."

"That's great, thanks," Warren said, his voice luxuriating.

Nick shuddered again, sensing the end of the universe—one blink of the eye and goodbye, a quick death, raw and barely violent. Nothing matters, he wanted to tell Himiko. Not a single thing, not really. In the long haul, it's all pointless. For all we know, it might already be too late.

So I'd rather not know who my date is.

17.

Nick hadn't expected to encounter Takashi at House of Pies; at least not before midnight, not while the Screw Your Roommate Dance was at full tilt. But there he was, by himself in a booth, smoking, flipping through a worn copy of *Spin* magazine that someone had left on the table. When Nick slid into the booth, taking the opposite seat, Takashi glanced up nonplussed, blew smoke from his nostrils, and then said, "Hello, Stranger, what are you doing here?"

"Good question," Nick replied, "so I'll ask the same."

"Wouldn't you like to know." Takashi scowled, tapping his cigarette with a finger and watching as ash fell to the tabletop.

"Actually, I would."

Takashi hesitated. Then he said, "My date sucked. Isn't your fault or anything, but it sucked ass."

Sucked ass?

"That's a little more information than I need to know," Nick joked.

But Takashi wasn't amused. He took a slow drag and shut the magazine, shaking his head.

"Come on, Tak, couldn't be any worse than my date with Himiko. Thanks a lot, by the way. You screwed me again."

"That's the idea, right? We're even."

"I doubt it. Anyway, how bad did it go?"

Takashi blew smoke at Nick.

"Bad. What else do you want to know?"

"I don't know. Everything, I guess."

A stupor enshrouded Takashi, as if his brain was having difficulty processing information. Where to begin? The condom and packet of lube that accidentally bounced from Warren Nathan's shirt pocket while they danced? How one of them stepped on the packet, bursting the contents underfoot, and both almost slipped in the mess.

"We looked like complete idiots, I swear. That was it—no more dancing for me. I had to leave."

So they went to Warren's dorm room. "I think I've got some wine," Warren had said. "Let's chill and watch TV or something." Except there wasn't any wine. And the video in the VCR wasn't a comedy or a drama or even a stupid sitcom, but ESPN bodybuilding competitions instead. The next thing Takashi knew, he was being kissed.

"I didn't stop him. Can't figure that, because the video was freaky and I was already disgusted by him and the whole thing was creepy. You want more?"

"Sure—"

What about Warren's tongue? A hard flesh dart shooting rapid-fire, jabbing at Takashi's gums. Or his lips? Wetter than wet, squishing against skin like a sponge.

That tongue again?

"He stuck it in my ear. Probably thought that was hot or something."

"Yuck."

"No romance or nothing. Just total gross."

"You have sex?"

"What do you think?"

Nick's eyes widened with surprise.

"I don't believe it, you did—"

Irritation crept over Takashi's face.

"Jesus, Nick, that was the last thing on my mind." He paused, shaking his head again. Suddenly muzak, loud enough to startle the patrons, blared from the overhead speakers in the diner. Beneath the noise came Takashi's low, quiet voice. "We only kissed—or he kissed me," he said. A few seconds went by before he added, "I just wanted out of there."

"Yeah, well—I—you know, I don't blame you," Nick stammered. "Think I'd be the same."

"Probably."

And that was it.

Takashi stamped his cigarette out on the table. Then he opened the magazine once more, turning the pages with little interest. Nick, feeling both culpability and satisfaction for his roommate's sour date, decided against mentioning what happened between him and Himiko—how they too had escaped the dance for a dorm room and alcohol. Peppermint schnapps and Cibo Matto playing on the stereo. The first kiss wasn't serious. The second was. He touched her breasts, she rubbed at the crotch of his jeans, until both fell back onto the bed laughing. Nick couldn't believe he went that far with her, because they were only friends and he wasn't that attracted to her.

"This is nuts," he told her.

"Are you hard?" she asked.

"Not really," he lied. "Are you?"

"Stupid, I'm dickless. You should know that by now." Then she said, "Can I see it?"

"No way!"

But he let her unzip his pants anyway. He put his arms behind his head as she worked his boxers down, and he grinned while she held his erect penis in her small hand; she gripped it at the base, squeezing, watching the skin turn dark-purple at the tip. "Weird." When his penis grew limp, she said it looked like the chest-burster in *Alien*, or like something that had been skinned.

"That's enough," he said, removing her hand. "You've exceeded your limit." Then he pulled his boxers to his waist. "Show me yours."

"Nope, don't think so, Nick. Sorry."

"Fair is fair."

"Sorry."

And for a while they lay together—Himiko's head on Nick's chest, her fingers stroking his sweater while they listened to the stereo. Then she propped on an elbow and stared at him.

"Guess what?"

"What?"

"I know someone who really likes you, Nick."

"Then you know something I don't."

"Yep," she said, "I do."

But he wasn't in the mood for gossip. He rolled on his side, facing her, touched her chin—and then, after some consideration, decided against kissing her.

Nick had no idea how long they remained sitting in the booth. But when they left House of Pies, the sky was brightening with the blue hue of dawn. Cool, humid gusts—the forefront of an impending storm—whirled about the parking lot in front of the diner. As they approached Nick's truck, Takashi suddenly stopped. "Go ahead," he said. "I feel like walking."

"Why?"

"That's how I got here, that's how I'll get home."

Nick nodded.

"Okay, whatever you want."

Takashi about-faced, saying, "Next year, I swear, let's go get drunk or take a road trip or something instead of the dance. We'll screw everybody else and not show up."

Nick laughed, unlocking the truck door. "That's a deal," he said. "I promise I won't stab you with my tongue either."

Takashi lifted a hand in the air, a kind of salute, and ambled forward. As Nick began climbing into the truck, Takashi's voice carried in the wind: "Well, if it's your tongue I don't care."

Nick smiled, glancing at the rearview. But Takashi had slipped from view. He turned around in the seat and looked—spotting only bits of trash, a plastic cup and crumpled newspapers, swirling in the parking lot.

Where'd you go, Tak?

He breathed heavily, then started the truck, sensing the fatigue in his body, knowing he'd be sound asleep before

The Shadow returned to HQ. And for a moment he listened—the engine groaning and rattling, the breeze whistling through the crack in the windshield.

TAKASHI

18.

WHEN DID Takashi realize it was Nick that he loved?

When did the idea of spending a lifetime with Stranger become The Shadow's principal fantasy?

Or perhaps it was just one infatuation replacing another: Before Nick there was Raji, a twenty-three year old fine arts major who Takashi had met in Study of Forms and Aesthetics (only later did he learn that Raji's real name was John). Soon the two became fast friends—taking long walks across campus at night, drinking coffee until dawn, discussing postmodernism for hours. Then it wasn't difficult falling in love with Raji; he was, after all, bisexual. "I possess both qualities equally," he told The Shadow. "Male and female, the feminine and the masculine." So attractive too, almost pretty, in a way delicate—with strawberry blond hair, blue eyes, Aramis designer glasses, very tall and very skinny and extremely pale, a smoker. He shunned material things—no computer, no TV, no car. "Humor," he said, "is an idleness I can't afford. A real artist must be serious, otherwise he isn't an artist. You must be disciplined, you must be selfless and completely free of ego." Meat was forbidden. Rice for breakfast and dinner was enough. "I learned this from the Buddhists who initiated me into their circle. But I am not a Buddhist—I prefer to remain ineffable."

And Takashi fell hard, for the first time. Someday, he knew, they would escape Houston as lovers. They would live somewhere far away—a farmhouse in the country, maybe a loft in Tokyo—and create masterpieces. They would be profound and influential artists, paradigm shifters; it was meant to be. But Raji couldn't love—at least that's what he said. "Boyfriends and girlfriends are a distraction, zapping the creative essence." This didn't stop The Shadow from trying (how many poems of tribute were written, how many bags of licorice-flavored jelly beans were left at Raji's doorstep?). And when Raji needed something—a few of The Shadow's acrylics, money for new brushes, help carrying his large self-portraits to and from his studio apartment—Takashi was happy to help, even if his generosity was accepted thanklessly.

"Don't trust him," Himiko had warned. "Don't ever trust bisexuals—they're all liars. What they say and do are always different things."

Still, they had kissed, The Shadow and Raji. They had hugged and held each other once in that studio apartment, bringing their clothed bodies together on a futon mattress.

Then, suddenly, it was over.

"I'm sorry," Raji said. "I'm tired—and I work in the morning."

The next day nothing was said, no mention was made. And how readily Raji pointed out—a week afterwards, over coffee and a blueberry scone at House of Pies—that if he could find the right guy or girl, a specimen of physical perfection, then his life would be a content one.

What's wrong with me? Takashi wanted to ask. Why not me? Instead he said, "I know how you feel."

"What an idiot," Stranger told The Shadow. "An arrogant fool. I don't like the way he treats you."

Himiko said, "He's disgusting, Tak. He's so pretentious. He doesn't deserve you."

But Nick and Himiko couldn't appreciate Raji like Takashi did: the guy was smart, a talented painter, interesting and eccentric and sensitive—and it was obviously a compliment when he said, "I only have sex with stupid people, Tak. That's why I won't with you—I think too much of you as a person. I don't want to hurt you."

"You can't hurt me."

"Don't say that—because I can."

"I don't understand."

How could The Shadow understand when he hadn't arrived at that place of enlightenment yet, that mystical plateau where twenty-three was the magic number?

"In about four years," Raji explained on more than one occasion, "you'll be where I am—then you'll understand what I'm talking about."

"In four years," Nick joked with Takashi, "if you're like him—still in college and waiting tables—then I'll do you a big favor and blow your head off. Anyway, I'd hate to see you end up such an insensitive jerk."

So at what moment did his heart get broken?

It happened in degrees, Takashi figured, little breaks here and there: the weekend trip to Galveston they had planned, canceled by Raji at the last minute ("I'm covering for someone at work"); the Rancid concert ticket The Shadow had bought as a favor (they were supposed to meet in front of the venue, but Raji never showed); the dinner at Star Pizza where, inexplicably, Raji politely excused himself from the table as their meal was served and never returned ("Had to get home," he said later, "just too much stuff to do—figured you'd understand.").

Until finally—when spotting Raji at House of Pies, holding hands with the female teaching assistant from their Art and the Mind seminar—Takashi's heart simply crumbled. Raji had seen The Shadow too, sitting there alone in a booth, staring at him—but no gesture was made, no smile or wave, just a furtive glance letting Takashi know that more important business was under way.

Then it was despair at HQ, with The Shadow languishing in his bed for an entire weekend while Nick tried consoling him: "Some people are unredeemable fucks, Tak. There's nothing you can do about it."

What a moron I am, Takashi thought repeatedly. How dumb.

But he wouldn't let himself cry, wouldn't call Raji or make himself anymore pathetic than he already felt. He'd have the weekend to angst—then he'd be done with it. When Stranger said, "You want me to pee on his door knob, maybe throw a rock through his window," Takashi couldn't help but wish he would.

"Nice of you to offer, except he's not even worth that, really."

And when Nick, in an effort to cheer The Shadow, danced around HQ with his boxer shorts on his head, strumming a tennis racket as if it were a guitar, and sang, "Look on the bright side, Mister Sad and Unhappy Man, you always got me and my three-legged dog and my brother named Bob and my sister who's my mom—," Takashi couldn't stop laughing.

"That's so stupid!"

"Second verse, same as the first—"

You're right, The Shadow reasoned, at least I have you—and your three-legged dog—

BING

19.

THANKSGIVING MORNING—and Susan was busy in the kitchen; she had been there, on and off, throughout the night, checking the turkey, wiping the counters, sweeping the floor, making pumpkin pies.

"Have you slept?" Bing asked.

"Yes," she replied, removing whipped cream from the freezer.

But Bing wondered if she was telling the truth. After all, her attire hadn't changed. Yesterday she wore a fringed shawl over her shoulders, a velvety blouse with black buttons and a plaid skirt. Today she wore the same. He imagined her resting on her made bed, dressed in the middle of the night, eyes shut but still awake; she wouldn't shift her body, wouldn't move her head, so as not to wrinkle her clothing or mess her hair or smear her makeup.

Now, in the kitchen, she looked immaculate. Just like a mannequin, Bing realized. Like a tidy lay figure that might fall to ruin if touched by the wrong hands. Her creations lined the countertop—fresh pumpkin pies sealed with cellophane, yams steaming within a covered dish, cut potato wedges waiting to be mashed, brown gravy simmering on the stove. Then there was the asparagus, the cranberry sauce, the oyster stuffing warming inside the turkey. There was the corn bread and apple-cheese biscuits and chocolate sticky rolls, all filling pans beside the stove.

How odd it was, Bing thought, that here stood the same woman who, years ago, railed against Thanksgiving and Christmas rituals, the original White Girl Disease, disrupting dinner parties with her loud opinions: "Please, the holidays are simply a bourgeois excuse to stuff one's self and then sit torpid in front of a television."

Valentine's Day?

"It's stupid. Who thought of creating a day where we tell the ones we love that we love them? Hallmark, that's who. Why not a day where we tell the ones we hate that we hate them? How about St. Retribution's Day? I could really get into that."

And hadn't she written a poem, a few short lines concerning her dislike of Thanksgiving dinners?

> *As if devoured by the meal she prepared—*
> *a pink thanksgiving turkey served half-cooked,*
> *a fallen pound cake—there is no comfort*
> *for her. She curses the bluntness of butter knives.*

The same woman? The poet and big mouth—chipping at frozen whipped cream with a fork, mumbling to herself amidst her holiday feast?

No. Not her. Not even close. That woman was dead. That woman didn't believe in God or watch television. That woman collapsed while teaching Yeats, an aneurysm at age thirty-two, almost killing her. Then a scalpel cutting around her crown, the scar from which—concealed now beneath her hair—had grown thin and white over time. And after a three-month coma and nearly two years of treatment, that woman failed to materialize again—this one emerged instead: strange and nervous, uninterested in books or poetry or the stars, a frail ghost haunting his wife's body for the past twenty-six years.

"Susan—?"

In between her stabs at the whipped cream, her voice hissed and whispered. Angry sounds, incomprehensible words. And that expression baring exhaustion; the face sunken and bloodless, the lips pinched and tight. Only the eyes prevailed, dark and reflective and alert, as if they were a youthful aberration among her other features—as though, if she had the strength or desire, she could peel away that tired aging mask and reveal her true self once more. For that was what surely hid somewhere below the surface.

"What can I do, dear?"

She fixed those eyes on Bing; lifting the fork, she pointed beyond him, indicating the dining room—where the table needed setting, the curtains opened.

"Of course," he said.

Before turning, a pain suddenly spread in his gut, twisting and sharp. He grabbed the counter for support and took a deep breath.

Diarrhea. Perhaps nerves.

He lowered himself to the kitchen floor and sat, waiting for the cramp to subside.

"Oh my," he said, clutching his belly.

And Susan, regarding her husband warily, looked away and continued hacking around the edges of the whipped cream with the fork—attempting to free the frozen chunk from its plastic container.

20.

IT WASN'T fair.

Could the fall semester have gone any worse? Bing had gotten little, if any, research done. He couldn't even remember how the days were spent, what became of the hours. In two weeks he'd be handing out student evaluations to the twelve survivors of Origins of the Universe (no doubt they'd slam him for bad behavior and tardiness and neglect). And the Trinity of Rot—"Bastards, all three!"— they had snubbed him at every turn. Four faculty lunches, one Halloween party, a catered dinner for the new graduate students, each event held without an invitation sent to him and Susan.

Betrayed again. Will it ever end?

"An oversight," Dr. Turman had explained. "No need to get all worked up, you know. Anyway, these are usually word-of-mouth affairs. I mean, you haven't been around that much—"

"Best avoid patronizing me," Bing replied. "I'm not stupid, I know what the score is with you people."

And don't forget Tong—pondering his supernova, getting endless amounts of attention and praise—who wouldn't return Bing's calls for some reason. How often had he phoned him? Four times a week, maybe more. But it was conversation he wanted, confidence, a friendly and reassuring voice.

"No, just tell him Bing Owen called again, please—and that it's important we talk when he gets free."

Was that asking too much, Tong?

Evidently.

At least there was Nick. Casey too. And now both were seated at his dining room table, waiting for Bing's return from the bathroom. Susan was there as well, eager to lead the prayer, silently reading in her *Living Bible* while Nick and Casey became acquainted.

"So you're a first year?"

"A sophomore."

"Oh. And you're a student of Bing's?"

"Yeah. In a way. Well, yes, I am—it's kind of an independent study thing—though I'm actually registered in his class. A bit complicated, I guess."

"I see—"

Bing could hear every word. In the middle of the table, set upon knitted pot holders, that hearty feast filled the room with its smells—the aromas finding him as he strained on the toilet.

Should've had them start without me, he thought. Should've insisted.

Since his stomach started acting up this morning, he'd made three trips to the bathroom. Each time he defecated blood. Buckets of blood, he imagined, squirting from his anus and discoloring the bowl. And once again—pants bunched at his ankles, a full wineglass near his shoes—he experienced the hot wetness pouring from within, splashing into water, some spattering back and hitting his bottom. The physics of diarrhea.

"Fucking perfect."

He sighed, reaching for the wineglass. It was almost laughable. On the one fall day when he should sense a modicum of happiness and well-being—there was blood. No, he didn't feel ill. Or dizzy. In fact, he felt fine—other than the cramps that seemed to come and go every hour or so.

But he was disconsolate. Today was Thanksgiving, he was among friends, and his own body was betraying him, preventing him from relaxing and having fun.

Should he go to the hospital?

No.

Or tell the others?

Absolutely not.

Phone a doctor from his bedroom phone?

Who would he call on a holiday anyway?

I can make it, he thought. At least until tomorrow.

If only someone would knock. Not the boy though. Maybe Susan, or Casey. If they'd knock and ask, "Are you okay?" Then he might let them in. He might show them what had spurted from his insides, that crimson waste so much thicker than toilet water. But they wouldn't come. They'd continue waiting.

In the dining room, Casey was telling his wife, "You've cooked a beautiful meal. Bet it tastes twice as good as it looks."

"Thank you," she said.

"Smells really great," Nick said.

"Yes, I suppose it does," she replied.

Bing, after abruptly returning the glass to the floor, wound toilet paper in his hand and for a moment there was no sound except the wineglass wobbling, rocking slightly at its narrow base. He wiped himself, all at once aware of the dampness seeping into the paper, and parted his thighs to gaze down into the bowl.

"Dammit—"

He let the paper fall from his hand, watching it become swallowed by the red water like a sinking ship.

What have I done to deserve this?

Then he closed his thighs, and with trembling fingers bent forward to still the wineglass, tipping it over instead.

21.

LEANING AGAINST the railing of his balcony, Bing said, "A most satisfying afternoon, I think—an affable evening too."

But—with the sounds of police sirens in the distance, the air smoggy and so cold that breath floated away like smoke—it was far from pleasant outside. Still, the lunch had gone well; both Nick and Casey ate their fill (Susan being quick to serve, making sure that the only bare plate on the table was her own). Then after the meal there was more wine—three bottles of merlot, uncorked and shared between the men in Bing's upstairs world. There was conversation, jokes, camaraderie as the day slipped into dusk, even as the last of the merlot was poured. Now standing beside Bing, empty wineglass in hand, Nick was buzzed, tired, and content.

"You're sleepy," Bing said.

Nick's gaze drifted over the balcony and down into the backyard.

"Kind of, I guess."

"Not surprised," Bing said. "You really packed it in. When I eat like that I'm usually exhausted. I'm done for."

Nick patted his stomach and smiled. He had swallowed more than his share of turkey, at least half a pumpkin pie, and sampled a bit of everything else that Susan had cooked. But he wasn't ungrateful or rude. In fact, he was brimming with politeness. "Thank you," he'd said after each serving. And before carrying his dishes to the kitchen sink (something he did of his own accord, bringing little blinks and an approving nod from Susan), he told his hosts, "You've no idea how long it's been since I've eaten this good. I really appreciate you having me."

"Haven't had you yet," Bing quipped. "You're the midnight snack."

Casey and Nick laughed.

But Susan frowned, regarding her husband with a stern face that wanted badly to speak: "You're shameless and stupid and I see right through you. I always have."

"That's funny," Bing said, amused at his own remark. "That's a hoot."

Yet as the afternoon progressed, as the merlot flushed his cheeks and numbed his feet, Bing's humor became more pointed, less friendly, with the meanest of his barbs reserved for Casey, each one taken from Ms. Bunny's act ("You say you can't climb plastic walls? How'd you get out of the abortion bucket then? That's rich!" "Son, the best part of you ran down your leg in the bathroom. I'm only kidding!" "No, I wouldn't say you were lazy, Casey. Well, actually, come to think of it, I would. I mean, you're so lazy that I bet if you woke up with nothing to do, you'd go to bed with it only half done. That's a good one!" "I'm sure your students don't think you're dull. I mean, you can still cut a fart, right?").

Seated on the couch with Bing, Casey handled the chiding as best he could, replying often with a grinning and passive, "Fuck you, Bing," or, "Very funny." But by his fifth glass he'd grown morose, ignoring most of what Bing was saying. Even when another toast was offered—"May your balls turn cubical and fester at the corners!"—he sipped his wine, attempting a half-hearted smile. And when Bing excused himself to go to the bathroom, Casey asked Nick, "So tell me—you like him? He's a good teacher for you?"

"Yeah, I think he is."

Nick sat cross-legged on the floor, in front of the coffee table, where he'd been reading Susan's book of poetry (*This Body's Broken Compass*) while Bing and Casey talked about the three T's—the Trinity, teaching, and Tong's incredible luck; subjects worthy of Bing's bane.

"It's been pretty interesting," Nick told Casey. "We've covered a lot of ground in a short period."

Casey cocked an eyebrow.

"I'm sure you have."

His voice was laced with the kind of innuendo Nick hated.

Then Casey rocked forward, lowering his tone, and said, "Want to know the truth, just between you and me—he's not that nice, you know. He's no saint, far from it, a million miles from it."

Nick stiffened as he took in Casey's fevered, drunken face, that ridiculous topknot, the black nose hairs curling from his nostrils: "Who is—?"

Taking a drink, Casey let the words sink in. *Who is*? Wearily he said, "Shit, that's right—who the fuck is. Hit it smack on the head, Nick-O. We're all creeps sometimes."

"I suppose," Nick said. "Well, at least some of us are."

Then with a heavy sigh Casey reclined, hoisting his drink, a meager toast in Nick's honor. And before Bing returned, he'd drifted off on the couch, head tilted back, a guttural snore rising from his throat—the wineglass held precariously at the rim by fingertips (there for Nick to rescue, to remove gently and set on the coffee table near Susan's book).

"Our friend has faded," said Bing, entering the room. He crossed behind the couch, pausing a moment to stare down at Casey's inert expression—the mouth hanging agape, the eyes shut tight. "Two little Indians left, you and me—"

Three bottles emptied? Was that right? And Nick wide awake, Casey passed out? Bing had expected otherwise. He had drunk with Casey over the years, knew that his colleague could match him shot for shot and still saunter from any bar like a sober man. So how surprising it was to find him unconscious, snoring fitfully, while Nick remained cognizant and sitting upright. That wasn't the way it was supposed to be.

Now on the balcony, Bing moved toward Nick with

twitching lips, as if about to whisper an important secret: "Well, you're more than welcome to stay here tonight, you know—if you've had too much, if you'd like to, that is. We've plenty of room, and it looks like Casey isn't going anywhere, so you might as well stay. Let's call it a Thanksgiving slumber party."

But Nick declined. He wasn't that drunk he explained. But he appreciated the offer. He appreciated everything. All the same, it was late and he needed to get going.

"Of course," Bing said. "Just so you'll know though, I consider you a friend more than a student. So if you ever need somewhere to sleep or escape to—not that you would, but if you do—my door is always open for you."

"That's nice of you. Thanks."

Bing held his gaze on him. The boy's cheeks, glowing from the alcohol or the cold, were burning and fresh.

"No, thank you—"

Then Bing hugged him; he pressed against Nick, pulling him close, bringing both hands against his boney shoulder blades. And Nick enveloped Bing, briefly squeezing him, saying once again, "I appreciate everything." If it weren't for the sudden grumbling in his gut, the churning pain reviving inside him, Bing could have held Nick all night, he would have never let him go. Perhaps, he thought, you feel the same.

SUSAN

22.

SHE HAD been teaching Yeats when the disabling headache filled her head, had been saying to her students: *Out-worn heart, in a time out-worn, come clear of the nets of wrong and right; laugh heart again in the gray twilight, sigh, heart, again in the dew of the morn—*
And even when she went to her knees—there in the classroom—even as the pain crippled her, the words were there.

> *Come, heart, where hill is heaped upon hill:*
> *For there the mystical brotherhood*
> *Of sun and moon and hollow and wood*
> *And river and stream work out their will;*

Then she collapsed, the chalk breaking in her fist, but remained conscious for a while—long enough to see the students rush around her, like wild things encircling prey, gazing down upon her with expressions more curious than frightened.
"Miss Owen? Are you okay?"
"Do you need help?"
Such drama, to fall while speaking verse, to end up on the floor with Yeats on the tongue. She tried talking to them, tried telling them something (I'm not ready to go yet, I have more, there's more to it), that last verse she loved so much.

> *And God stands winding His lonely horn,*
> *And time and the world are ever in flight;*
> *And love is less kind than the gray twilight,*
> *And hope is less dear than the dew of the morn.*

And then she was gone.

NICK AND BING

23.

AN *A*, a pen set, a jar of homemade chutney, a plane ticket, a full-sized bed with a comforter; the presenting season.

"For you—"

At semester's end—without any homework, without any tests, without anything except required attendance— Bing gave Nick an *A* in Origins of the Universe. Then, as a Christmas gift, he gave Nick a Webster-Julian pen set: "Wouldn't advise chewing on them, they'll break your teeth. Anyway, Merry Christmas, Nick—you're a wonderful young man."

How grateful Nick was for the present, how pleased (though he already owned a similar pen set, a birthday gift from his grandfather). "I don't know what to say. This means a lot. Thanks, Bing."

And how surprised Takashi looked when, on the evening he left Houston to spend the holiday recess with his mother in Amarillo, Nick found him standing in front of their dormitory and placed the green velvet Webster-Julian box in his right hand.

"Merry Christmas, Tak. You can do sketches or something with these—or whatever."

But Nick had violated their agreement, the one made last year after both became disgusted by the Yuletide's blatant commercialization (all those red and green and silvery decorations adorning shopping center windows and the street poles near the Galleria, appearing before unsold Halloween masks could be marked down for clearance): *No Christmas gifts will be swapped between The Shadow and Stranger, ever!*

"Oh, no, you're not supposed to—"

"Don't worry about it. It's nothing."

Still, Takashi welcomed the pens, feeling gratified by Nick's thoughtfulness. And while waiting for the taxi that would transport him to the airport, he reached inside his backpack, dug deep, and retrieved a mason jar of chutney.

"It's not much, I know. But I want you to have it—you know, the idea that counts and all that."

Homemade chutney—reeking of vinegar and spices, a red ribbon adorning the lid— given as a Christmas present to all members of G.L.A.M. (Gay & Lesbian Association at Moss) who helped paint banners for National Coming Out Day.

Nick shook the jar, watching the contents move around like car oil.

"Thanks, Tak. Are you sure?"

"Absolutely."

When the taxi arrived, Nick draped an arm over Takashi's shoulders, pulled him close and said, "Have a safe trip home, okay?"

Takashi patted Nick's side.

"You too. See you next year, Stranger."

"Maybe," Nick replied, smiling.

Then a quick handshake, a car door shutting, a muffler blowing exhaust as the taxi sped off. The Shadow had escaped Moss, but Stranger remained, holding chutney and sensing the first rumblings of loneliness; this on the last day of finals, on the day prior to the dorms closing until mid January. In approximately thirty-six hours, he'd also be leaving Moss, taking a flight to snowy Colorado for the break; the ticket home being a surprise from his mother and stepfather (the reservations set thirty days in advance, guaranteeing a cheaper holiday rate): "So you got no excuse, kiddo. You're coming whether you want to or not."

His mother had forgotten that the dorms closed soon after finals, had failed to consider that fact when purchasing the plane ticket. Nick had too. But he wasn't bothered—

even as the lobby of his dormitory became desolate, as fewer and fewer bodies passed him in the corridors, and the sidewalks and walkways of Moss took on a forsaken quality at dusk.

What to do? Nick wondered. Where to go?

Classes were finished. Takashi was gone. Himiko was gone. The library glowed with fluorescence, but the doors were locked. Tomorrow he'd find somewhere else to stay, a motel for a night, or maybe he'd save money by sleeping at the airport, find a bench near his terminal and camp there. Or maybe he'd kill time at House of Pies, claim a booth for twenty-four hours and caffeinate with a book.

Or maybe—

Nick phoned Bing from HQ.

"Just wanted to say thanks again for the present, and if you're not busy or anything I was hoping I could stop by tomorrow and give you and Susan a gift. It's nothing much but—"

The chutney sat on Nick's dresser.

"Don't ask," Bing said, his voice reveling, made warm and deep with brandy. "We'd be delighted to see you— perhaps around lunchtime. Noon. How's that?"

"That's good for me."

"Fantastic. Lunch it is. To be honest, Nick, I expected you to be on the road in that beast truck of yours. I was thinking about you moments ago, thinking, I bet he's already left town. Then the phone rang. Very odd, don't you think?"

"Yeah, strange. Except I'm kind of stuck here. At least until Friday."

"Really?"

"Yes."

Then Nick explained everything. He mentioned the plane ticket, the dorm closing, that he'd probably get a motel the following night.

"Nonsense," Bing said. "You'll be staying here. I won't

have it any other way. You'll get the guest room. Christ, that's what guest rooms are for, right?"

"Are you sure? I mean, I don't want to intrude or anything."

"I insist, Nick. Understand? I insist. Your company is as good as any gift you could offer us. I'm serious."

What a welcoming guest room it was: a full-sized mattress—much better than a bunk bed, much better than a motel mattress, the best place in the world for a young man to rest his body—with a comforter so thick and cozy and encompassing that sometimes Bing slept there instead of in his own bedroom, the other guest room at the end of the hall.

"My promise, Nick—you'll sleep well before your flight. So no more talk of motels, okay?"

"Okay," Nick said. "I appreciate it, Bing. Thanks."

"No thanks required," Bing replied. "That's what friends are for."

The next morning, Nick dumped the contents of his backpack on his bed, clearing space for the clothing he'd be taking on the trip. Underwear. Socks. Four shirts (no doubt his mother would be getting him more clothes for Christmas). He'd leave his Jnco jeans, bringing only his green cargo pants which he'd wear. In the side pocket where he usually kept his pens, he packed his toothbrush and comb and anti-perspirant deodorant. On top of his clothes he placed Bing's book. Beside the book he wedged the jar of chutney, a note attached reading: *To Bing and Susan. Merry Christmas, Nick.* And before evacuating HQ, he scanned the room, making sure nothing important was left behind.

Plane ticket?

Got it.

Wallet?

Got it.

Lights off? Computers unplugged?

Check.

Then he wandered from the room, locking the door, and headed down the vacant corridor—whistling "Silver Bells" and entertaining the idea that he might be the last man on earth.

24.

BING'S PROSTATE had grown.

"Not much smaller than a baseball," his internist said.

"Is that normal?"

"No. Normal is a chestnut, normal is a Ping-Pong ball."

That explained the blood in the semen, the piss that sometimes dribbled and burbled out.

"Any burning when you urinate?"

"No."

"Problems with erections?"

"No, fortunately."

"Well, when you catch buzzing, it's probably just a fly. Of course, if you're inclined to think it's a wasp, or even a killer bee, then have a field day—worry yourself sick if you want."

Antibiotics were prescribed.

"Should do the trick."

Only a fly, Bing thought. That's all.

But he began shitting blood in November.

That was when he began uttering to himself, "Killer bees," while envisioning cancer cells swarming with long stingers, poking away at his guts.

So he sought a second opinion.

"Gastroenteritis."

And a third opinion.

"Gastroenteritis."

Then it was high-priced antibiotics, labeled with the warning: MAY CAUSE DROWSINESS. ALCOHOL MAY INTENSIFY THIS EFFECT. USE CARE WHEN OPER-ATING A CAR OR DANGEROUS MACHINERY. But the warning went unheeded, the tablets often washed down with wine or brandy or bourbon, sometimes coffee. Nevertheless, by finals week he was in the clear. No more blood, no more drippy piss, no more tainted sperm, no more Origins of the Universe (at least for a month). So on the day Nick arrived in his clunky truck, backpack in hand, Bing considered himself a saved man.

"Howdy howdy!"

He met Nick in the driveway, greeting the boy with a high five, a stylish salutation in Bing's mind; how suddenly youthful and sober and alive he felt. Inside, he bounded up the stairs, Nick following. With wild sweeping motions, he threw open the curtains in the guest room, allowing sunlight to spill across the floor, to cut over the mattress and fleecy comforter. Then in the kitchen, as Susan hid in her bedroom, he made lunch—sliced leftover turkey, iced tea, fruit salad, the chutney gift as a condiment—talking all the while, speaking in a gleeful, frenetic way which amused Nick.

"Lord, I hate Christmas, I really do. Maybe if I had kids, maybe if there was any family still living I wanted to see. You know, one Christmas my grandmother bit me, that's true—senile old cunt, not a nice woman. Another Christmas, my father stumbled drunk into the tree and toppled it, stomped his boots on my presents, crushed my plastic Zap gun and my toy taxicab with actual working headlights—Merry Christmas, right? Ho ho ho and humbuggery, I say!"

So all that afternoon and evening, Nick and Bing drank merlot in the upstairs study; Bing chatting away, Nick listening. What a sot Bing was, downing most of the wine himself—"a very nice vintage, good stuff"—as if it flowed freely from the tap and wasn't an expensive brand from Chile; continually removing the cork, replenishing the glass, eventually leaving the bottle empty, excusing himself for a moment—down the stairs, into the kitchen, returning—two unopened bottles, one in each hand. Bing and his secret stash. The second time he excused himself, Nick gave him a worried stare, with the complete beauty of his blue eyes: You've had enough, you'll get sick, I'm not having anymore. But what returned his stare? A grin and a wink and a flare of nostrils; Bing placating Nick with a silly face, so that the boy had no choice but to flash a smile and to feel foolish for having displayed concern.

Bing went and returned again. What a sot: bumping up the stairs with another bottle, weaving into the study and laughing for no apparent reason, as if he was going happily insane. Watching as Nick stood and yawned the words, "I'm pretty exhausted, guess I better crash." And what was Bing trying to say? Clutching the bottle neck in a fist, wet lips twisting while uttering something odd beneath his foul breath; his face was like a huge tomato. You're wasted, Nick thought, pausing to catch the meaning of that whispery slur. What are you telling me?

"Goodnight, Saint Nick. Sleep tight. Goodnight—"

Now Nick was gone, already among the mountains and chill of Colorado, and Bing—on his balcony with Pussy, drink in hand—missed the boy's presence, his polite charm, the way he sometimes brushed the hair from his face while talking. But they'd see each other again, Bing knew; not the end of something, he thought, just the beginning: Perhaps he misses me as well, looks forward to returning, to finding me waiting for him there at the airport terminal.

"No, you won't call a cab," he'd told Nick that morning, "nor will you take that truck—you'll have to park it and that'll cost plenty. I'll deposit you at the airport myself."

"Really, you've already done enough—"

"Nonsense."

Was this the same day? Had it been only hours ago that Nick climbed into Bing's Buick? That Bing, wishing to seem paternal, rested a palm on Nick's shoulder and asked, "You ready? Got your ticket?"

"Yep."

"All right, I guess we're set."

Then along the highway they went, amongst cars and pickups and vans that sped southwards—as if, Bing envisioned, the drivers were fleeing Houston before disaster struck the city. The profiles of holiday travelers—restless children in the backseat, fathers and mothers up front—zoomed by the Buick, one vehicle after another, like variations on the same theme.

Where were they all going?

Past the weathered shotgun shacks on the cradle of the interstate, the expanse of shopping centers, the endless urban sprawl that stretched toward NASA and Galveston Island—places where rural communities and towns once existed, now consumed by their larger neighbor—and the oil refineries spitting fire into the clear sky.

Because they all had somewhere else to go? Like Nick—who wouldn't let Bing park his Buick at the airport, arguing that it was better to drop him off: "It'll save us both time." Even though there was a traffic jam at the Passenger Pick Up—hazard lights blinking, suitcases being loaded into trunks, embraces and kisses and happy families.

Bing said, "You know, I don't mind going in with you. What if your plane is delayed, or cancelled?"

But Nick wouldn't hear of it. He was ready to leave, offering simply a handshake and a hurried, "I owe you for everything, Bing. Take care. I'll phone you when I get my return flight schedule." Then from the Buick he clambered, holding his backpack, weaving between cars, approaching an airport entrance, turning briefly to wave.

Then gone.

Somewhere else. But not for Bing. Back along the highway, by the strip malls and refineries, his chest tightened as if to remind him: You are alone. You have always been alone. With your supernovae and gastroenteritis and damaged wife. Your upstairs world, your balcony.

Somewhere else.

But not for Susan, surely in her bedroom, praying for deliverance, until sleep found her in the hours before dawn. "Redemption," Brother Van Horn repeated on her TV. *Redemption* read odd notes left on napkins in the kitchen, on the pad beside the downstairs telephone. Susan's word: redemption. Had Bing pondered it while leaning into the balcony railing, there in the night, longing for a boy he hardly knew? No. Still, he'd remained with his wife all those years (she didn't need him anymore—as long as God resided downstairs, Bing was pointless). He had lost his lover Marc (the other boy, that painful remembrance, who had made real love seem so tangible). Now, Nick—was there any repurchase in knowing him, in desiring him? And if he had not pondered the possibility of redemption, then had he perhaps prayed for a sign—something telling, something that might bring him closer to the boy? Of course.

And tomorrow, Bing would find a pair of flannel boxer shorts in the guest room; discarded by Nick after his morning shower, tossed upon the comforter and forgotten. Another gift, nicer than chutney. Yet no hint of the boy was apparent, no distinguishing odor or taste (that didn't stop Bing's tongue and nose from exploring the cotton, didn't prevent him from burying his face into the crotch of the shorts while fumbling with his zipper). But tonight, alone on the balcony, he wanted to cry.

"I owe you for everything," Nick had said.

Yes, Bing thought, you do.

SPRING

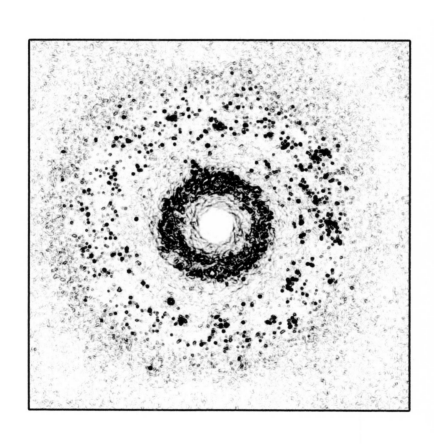

NICK AND BING

25.

THE PIG Slice, remaining open until 12:30 a.m. on January 1st, offered patrons a complimentary slice and a cup of beer at midnight. But for Nick the New Year arrived with a free small beer-crust cheese pizza ("Thanks, Mom") and a pitcher of Coors ("Thanks, Dad")—the late night meal filling him up while a snowstorm powdered Durango, blanketing the roads and mountains, smoothing the land into panoramas of white which, as the skies began clearing before dawn, glowed pristinely beneath a full moon. The following morning, Nick sat in the living room of his parents' home, still awake and buzzed, a quilt draped over his shoulders, and wrote on a sheet of loose-leaf paper:

> *I am the Dragon, flamboyant animal,*
> *no friend of the Dog, seeking only*
> *the company of Rats and Monkeys*
> *in this place where I am a lost pilgrim,*
> *a Dragon by birth, just another stranger*
> *seeking my own kind, instead of Dogs.*

It wasn't a very good poem; in fact, Nick hated it. Still, he had to start with something. A Dragon? Rats and Monkeys? He wasn't sure what the stanza meant—so he crumpled the paper, tossed it on the floor (isn't that what real writers did when the words came out all wrong?), and began again. Now he had to focus. He had to mean what he wrote. No tricks, no gimmicks. He had to be honest. No dragons, no dogs, no rats or monkeys.

> *My brain is empty,*
> *I cannot think.*

As I scrawl this poem
My ideas they do stink.
I'm not a lover,
I'm not a fighter.
Fucking hell,
why be a writer?

Yet Nick had always wanted to be a writer. Even as a child he entertained himself with fiction (Hardy Boys, Sherlock Holmes) and wrote stories (the plots based on movies he liked—*Psycho, Star Wars, The Horror of Dracula*). The first thing he committed to paper was entitled *The Haunted House.* Actually, he was too small to write a word, so his mother jotted down the spooky tale; regardless, the accompanying illustrations were all his—the dark house on the hill (looking more like random scribbles than a house) and the bloody elephant that haunted the place (more scribbles rendered in red ink). Later, while in high school, he dabbled with poetry for his English Composition class, creating dull odes to the countryside and the evening skies. Then, as a freshman at Moss, he contemplated the novel he'd someday write, a rich narrative about collegiate adventures and a protagonist who escaped a stifling small town and came to Houston and fell in love and eventually grew into a distinguished man who wrote books; it would be an epic, at least a thousand pages, perhaps longer.

Nevertheless, the notion of becoming a novelist hadn't occupied his thoughts lately, not that fall at Moss, not until he found himself at the downtown library in Durango, bored and cold, searching for an interesting book which might ease the holiday doldrums: How much digital cable could one person watch? How much MTV before the dance parties and beautiful faces forged a burning question mark—did this life offer more than fashion? But there was little else to ponder at his parents' place (aside from those lousy Harlequin romance novels his mother loved, or those

Tom Clancy thrillers his stepfather read before bed). So he wandered into the library, eyes scanning the shelves, searching for something new. Like *The Catcher in the Rye*, except different. Like *On The Road*, except tighter. Like Whitman, except modern. Like—

This Body's Broken Compass.

Susan's book, appearing right in front of his face, that same collection of poetry he'd flipped through in Bing's upstairs study. How strange to have discovered it in Durango, so many miles from Houston. How even stranger that the author—she looked so much younger and happier on the dust jacket—had cooked him meals and led the Thanksgiving prayer. And in the library, while his parents made pizza down the street and children played outside in the snow, Nick read her poems once again, confounded by the connection—this was the same woman he knew, the wife of Bing. Such ominous lines—*The house is not a house, nor a home, but a vessel for feeble grief we covet like precious cargo*—and he could envision her, in that house not a house, moving about the kitchen, washing dishes, saying nothing. What had happened to her? And Bing? When were the poems written, and why had she stopped writing? Where were her other books?

Nick leaned against a bookcase, reading, remembering now what he'd let himself forget: He desired his own book, a novel or stories or poems, in a library somewhere. Just to write, to become a writer, as simple as that—simpler than stealing Susan's book, than removing the protective coat from the dust jacket, finding the magnetic security strip taped along the binding—simpler than walking out of the library on New Year's Eve, her book zipped up inside his ski vest.

That evening, he called Moss' Registration System Via Phone, changing his spring schedule, dropping Greek Architecture and Survey of the Galaxy, adding Intro Writing of Poetry and Intro Writing of Fiction. Then he announced to his mother, "I'm going to write."

"About what?"

"I don't know. Lots of stuff."

She cocked an eyebrow, smiled at one end of her mouth, as if to say, "Whatever—and next week you'll be a lawyer."

"I'm serious," Nick wanted to tell her. "I'm as serious as a heart attack." Instead he phoned Takashi in Amarillo, wishing him a Happy New Year, and then mentioned, "By the way, Tak, I've made up my mind—I'm going to write."

"That's great!" Takashi said. "I'm glad you finally decided."

Because they'd talked about Nick's future at HQ, on those nights when both felt directionless and worried. Often Stranger told The Shadow that he admired him for being a painter, for following his dream, even though it was difficult to make a living in the art world. So Nick knew Takashi would be happy for him, that The Shadow wouldn't cock an eyebrow, thinking, "Yeah, right, a writer—good luck!"

He also knew that Bing would be pleased for him, that the old guy would say, "That's delightful," or, "Fantastic, Nick, really wonderful." But on the day he returned to Houston, Bing frowned when he heard the news, asking, "Are you finished with the heavens then?"

"No way," Nick replied. "That's the awesome thing about writing, you can use everything. It's all grist for the wheel."

"The mill," Bing corrected. "Grist for the mill."

They were seated at Bing's dining room table, eating a late lunch (grilled cheese sandwiches, Pringles, milk), and Nick saw disappointment claim the man's face, a somber expression that suggested grave thoughts: With glassy eyes focused on the tabletop, Bing nibbled his sandwich, exhaling heavily from his nostrils as he chewed. Suddenly Nick felt disappointed too (wasn't Bing supposed to congratulate him, to perhaps retrieve a bottle of wine so toasts could be made?). To lighten the mood, Nick considered mentioning the copy of Susan's book he'd liberated from the Durango Public Library; instead he ate his sandwich silently, glancing occasionally toward the kitchen, where he hoped Susan might soon materialize. But there was no sign of her—no prayer pamphlets left strategically on the table, no television rumbling in her bedroom. Then it was as if Susan never existed, and, Nick imagined, if he went to remove her book from his backpack it wouldn't be there. Eventually, between bites, he said, "Maybe I'll write poems about black holes and pulsars and stuff like that. I can come over every week and show them to you."

"Maybe—" Bing replied, his mouth full, then he continued chewing, doing his best at pretending Nick wasn't seated across from him.

And Nick sensed he'd somehow joined Susan, vanishing now within Bing's house, becoming a ghost. Am I here? he wondered. Did I just fly in from Colorado? Was the snow real and the air crisp and the stars so bright at night, so clear and sparkling and abundant? Did I greet the New Year with a sheet of paper and bad poetry?

Bing sighed. He raised his head and lowered his sandwich. "You'll make a fine writer," he said. "Yes, I believe you'll be fantastic."

"Thank you," Nick said, relief saturating his voice.

"You'll show me your poems, right?"

"Yes."

"Good," Bing said, winking once with his left eye. "I'm certain a drink or two is in order, don't you?"

"Sure, if you want—"

Bing nodded emphatically.

"Oh, I want. I want very much."

Then Bing winked again—and Nick winked back.

26.

THE HOUSE *is not a house*—

In Bing's study, Nick uttered that line of Susan's poem—"nor a home, but a vessel for feeble grief"—slurring the words, his lips stained red with wine. Bing yawned (they had been discussing great poets and writers), then he checked his watch, saying, "You should probably be going, I think, before you're too hammered to drive," because the boy's company had become tiresome (too much boring chitchat about Whitman and Hemingway, Dickinson and Salinger).

What about physicists? What about the electroweak theory of the combined electromagnetic and *weak* interactions? Well—?

"You're right, I'm zonked. I should unpack and crash."

So goodnights were exchanged, firm handshakes traded (Nick bent forward beside the couch, grasping Bing's hand). Thanks for the lunch, thanks for the wine, thanks for going to the airport and for babysitting the truck. Thanks again. And as the boy wandered from the room, backpack dangling at his side, Bing stretched lengthwise across the couch and sipped at his glass.

"No, the house is not a house," he told Pussy when she crawled into his lap.

Nor a prison, he thought. Or at least less of a prison than the classroom, than the token spring seminar the Trinity had bequeathed him: Survey of the Galaxy, same as Origins of the Universe but with a different title.

"A turd by any other name, Pussy, is still a turd, you know."

Of course, droves of students would drop the class. The evaluations would be harsh. But he didn't care, he really didn't; his heart wasn't in the game any more (the very idea of teaching or doing essential research in his field made him nauseous), so the Trinity could have their way. Anyway, he had already decided, without a doubt, that this would be his last semester at Moss: Then you won't have Bing to humiliate, I swear. Be finished with me, and you monsters will turn on each other—McDouglas will bite Rosenthal, Rosenthal will fang Turman, Turman will sink his teeth into McDouglas—like some venomous three-headed serpent fighting for the right to devour its own tail.

And filthy Joy Vanderhoof?

She would fall as well. Her loyalty to the bitch McDouglas would get her sacked. With Bing out of the picture, he figured, it would be only a matter of time before she hanged herself, before she whispered an anti-Semitic remark regarding Rosenthal ("Ever get this feeling Hitler had the right idea?"), before she joked hatefully within earshot of Turman ("Know what G.A.Y. stands for? Got Aids Yet.").

"She'll wreck herself, Pussy baby. She's too dumb to avoid it."

But he wouldn't be there when Joy imploded. After this semester, he'd retire, sell the house, and move far away. Maybe go to Arizona where he'd put a telescope on a hill somewhere and watch the heavens among towering saguaros. Or maybe he'd leave Susan the house and the bank account, keeping for himself Pussy and the Buick, a few books, some clothing. Then he'd hit the road—"Adios, you bastards!"—because life, he believed, was too short for the kind of misery Moss dealt. Plus, he wasn't getting younger; another year in Houston, occupying the house not a house, and his prostate would balloon again, his insides would once more leak blood into his underwear. Another stagnant year—and he would die.

Bing lifted his wine glass toward the ceiling.

A toast to new beginnings, to the end of academics for Bing Owen.

A toast to Pussy, content in his lap, sleeping with him at night when others would not.

A toast to Nick, that lovely young man: Yes, he thought, I'd be dead already if it weren't for you and your visits and your interest in me.

Regrettably, the boy was no longer Bing's student (Survey of the Galaxy couldn't compete with Intro to Writing Poetry), but Nick would come around once a week. They'd drink together, and Bing would read his poems (God knows they won't be good. How could they be?), never mentioning what he discerned as truth—writers were born writers; the aptitude wasn't emergent, blossoming like some whim between Christmas and New Year's Day.

"Should've stuck with me, Nick. You're really an astronomer, my student and partner—"

Nonetheless, he planned on praising the boy's talent, telling him that his verse was tight, insightful, almost transcendent. Nick would appreciate the compliments (the young were always content with bones of tribute). But Bing wouldn't tell him that poetry did little for people, that it didn't help husbands and wives, it didn't prevent aneurysms or save marriages. And, as far as Bing knew, the only people enjoying verse these days were the poets, and even then it was usually their own work—all that self-important blather spewed in coffee shops or book stores, reeking of "I'm different" and "I'm so much more in-tune than you are."

"Give me a break—"

All the same, a toast to the great poets.

A toast to real poetry—a full glass of merlot, Pussy's kneading paws, Mahler's 9th coming from the stereo, starbursts and colossal galactic explosions. And Nick's discarded boxer shorts (how clean a boy he was, how odorless). Boxer shorts easily bunched in one liver-spotted hand, excellent for catching semen—there's poetry in that, perhaps.

But not in this.

He took Susan's book from the coffee table.

"No, not in this—"

The lies of the Ice Queen disguised as art, written when she was the Snow Princess. Each poem was filed in memory; flipping the book open to a random page, he scanned the first line—*In the weeks following the funeral,*—and the rest he recited with eyes closed:

he had fallen six times,
chipping a tooth once,
as he went to grab her.
If she were upset,
he knew,
he needed just to hold her.
Since their only child died,
when she was bothered or sad,
he understood
that anything he had to say
wouldn't help;
he became nervous and attentive,
would put his arms around her waist.
On more than one occasion
she had been surprised in the kitchen
as his long fingers
suddenly folded across her stomach
from behind
when he was supposed to be at work.
Sometimes he would carry her
into their bedroom
if he suspected she needed more than a hug—
just lay her on the sheets
and undress her
without saying a word,
and put his body into her body,
offering himself
as a small consolation.

Holding the book by the spine, Bing snapped it shut.

What myth. What untruth. There had been no child, no funeral. He never carried her, she would never have let him.

See, Nick, poetry books are the same as fibs. Perfect for throwing across the room, for startling Pussy, for making a racket.

A toast to Susan.

"You fooled them, didn't you? You lied with words and they believed you because they wanted to."

He flung the book, sending it smashing against a wall, where, like a bird careening into an office building window, it fluttered briefly while dropping to the floor.

"Good riddance!"

Then Bing raised his glass.

A toast—

SUSAN

27.

We look at each other,
hear each other,
and what we understand
is just wrong.
We've been here before.
It's time to call it quits again,
and this time I mean it.
We'll continue as friends, of course.
Even best friends.
But we're like two old soldiers,
worn and beaten
in another pointless war,
suffering with sadness
from the damage we've seen
and inflicted.

Anyway, I can't compete
with your true lovers—
supernovae, wormhole theory,
cosmic rays, dark dark matter.
Small hugs and back rubs mean nothing
where the universe is concerned.
And, truth be known, my bedfellows
give you no comfort or satisfaction;
the marked pages and broken spines
of Snodgrass, Beckett, Sexton,
and Yeats don't exist for you
in your world.
I'm sorry for that.
But, then again, as you've said,
everything is physics.

There are no words, I think,
for this kind of loss.
I'm babbled out and muted.
I want to say what it is
that eludes me,
but my attempts
are gibberish.
You've seen me cry too much
this past weekend.
And we're both defeated now.
Three years.
Can you believe it?
Three years we've been married.
So I'll never be your ideal mate,
or you my savior.

When you leave the house,
I worry about your safety,
because your driving scares me.
But I can't speak.
I wish to be silent.
The sound of my voice
is like paper tearing,
knuckles popping
over an open microphone,
creating static.
What you tell me sounds like nonsense.
Since when has science
ever had anything to do
with Love?

Remember that I wrote this once:

> *How to explain the lengths of us?*
> *The occasion of our meeting*

some time ago.
When spring, with a distant sun,
held forth,
I caught your name,
repeated it twice to myself,
that night holding it in my sleep.

To explain the lengths of us
to a stranger,
to even a close friend—
what's the purpose?
Try explaining God,
or some blessed satori,
the words of an unwritten poem,
the strains of an unmade instrument,
a dead language never found,
the drunken reverie of a lost man,
the umbra and penumbra of sunspot pairs.

Simply, to them,
I say,
when, a time ago,
I heard your name spoken,
said it twice to myself,
and made it mine.

Now:

I've taken the ring from my finger
and put it away.
It is, I suppose, symbolic of something.
There are two of us in this house—
one of them is me, the other is you.
I'm at the desk in my office.
You are somewhere else,
and the door is shut between us.

BING

28.

AT ERIC'S Rotisserie, Bing sat outside by himself, nursing white zinfandel beneath the large sunshade that jutted from the center of his table, while a blustery wind roamed across campus—swirling dead leaves and bits of trash around the chairs and tables, flapping the awnings on the massive umbrellas. The weather kept the patio abandoned, and Bing preferred it that way—no chatty couples nearby, no loud-mouth students talking about sports, or, even worse, popular music. On this chilly afternoon, he didn't care that he was alone. He didn't care that he'd left his coat in his office. For a moment, he almost didn't mind that his head wasn't quite screwed on tightly today, or that Dr. Turman had requested a few minutes of his time.

But how'd I forget my coat?

"Another drink, sir?"

The waiter—a tall, skinny kid with brown curly hair, a long nose, wide eyes—stood beside the table, shivering some and rubbing at his forearms, shaking below the waist as if his feet were warming on hot coals. His sudden appearance relieved Bing, who had just then emptied his glass.

"Yes, another—"

"Right on," the kid said, oozing fake enthusiasm. He took the glass and about-faced, moving forward into the wind.

You're a pest, Bing thought. Buzz buzz.

He watched the waiter's ass, compact and firm, riding high in black slacks, observed the manner in which the kid's hair got attacked by the breeze, the curls twisting like dark tendrils. His own hair, Bing knew, was getting mussed as well, fluffed and puffed in all directions—the hair of a mad professor, he imagined; the crazy one, that's what the Trinity believed.

So let them.

"Stupid bastards."

Anyway, he wouldn't be an isolated example in his field. There were others, more extreme nuts, populating the world of astrophysics (the Harvard physicist who was arrested for jogging naked, the cosmologist in Japan who hanged himself with a cucumber stuffed in his rectum). Still, Bing believed, he wasn't terribly unhinged. But these days the medication for his stomach—coupled with his intake of merlot, a bad combination—made him feel less grounded, somewhat fuzzy; it was difficult remembering, burdensome to put details together.

Perhaps it's better as a pigeon, he thought, pecking around like this one near my table, looking for scraps. Or a squirrel, scampering out there in the grass. Then I wouldn't forget, I wouldn't remember.

But who could blame him? His internist hadn't told him anything; the man didn't say, "You drink too much, you take your pills, and you'll forget everything. Your behavior will be altered, you'll do something you regret and no soul will see that it wasn't your fault, that the culprits are pills and booze." Now he wished someone had explained the side effects, rather than expecting him to memorize the warning label. If someone had pounded the secondary reactions into his skull, he might have avoided his pills last night altogether.

How many had he swallowed?

He wasn't certain: Did I have you yet, pill? No? Yes? Well, one more, just in case—

And a little more wine. A little more. Never mind that Bing taught in the morning. Never mind that the spring semester had been in full swing for almost two weeks and Nick hadn't called or offered him any poems to read. So he dialed the boy's number, almost every evening, reaching no one. But he didn't leave a message on the answering machine. He didn't say, "Hey, kiddo, this is Bing. Give me a call when you get in, okay?" He didn't say, "I miss you and you're my friend, and I'd like to see you. Why haven't you called me, please do."

Instead, he listened to the outgoing message, gathering comfort from Nick's recorded voice: "Hey, Nick and Tak aren't here at the moment. Well, actually, we are, but we don't want to talk to you because we've got important things to do—like, you know, toss dwarfs and slap our women around. So leave your name and number after the beep and we'll add you to the growing list of family and friends we don't call back." Then Bing waited for the beep, and he wouldn't hang up until a few seconds of silence had been recorded, manifesting as a blinking red light at HQ.

Still, if Nick had stopped by the house sometime or called, then Bing wouldn't have phoned him again last night; he wouldn't have spoken to the boy, or ended up spending the next day rummaging through his memory for what had transpired—dialing Nick's number, Nick answering for once. But he didn't want to recall anything either, because there was fear and pain in remembering. Too many pills, he reasoned, and wine, not my fault, wouldn't have called him otherwise. Then he wouldn't be at Eric's now, in the cold, studying the leaves and squirrels and pigeons, hoping to forget everything. He'd be at home or seated in his office. He'd be more like himself.

He'd be wearing his coat.

29.

EARLIER THAT afternoon in the hallway of the Astro-Science Building, Dr. Turman had stopped Bing in the hallway, asking, "Can I have a word with you in my office?"

A word?

Bing raised an eyebrow.

I've got a word for you: cocksucker.

"Sure thing, cocksucker," Bing wanted to tell him. But he didn't. Instead he walked beside Turman, engaging in small talk about the weather.

"Suppose we're in for rain."

"Yes, yes, I think so—"

Once inside his office, Turman closed the door and asked Bing to take a seat. Then he stood in front of his desk, towering over Bing, and folded his arms, saying, "Is there some problem?"

Is there some problem?

"That's more than one word." Bing counted them off with his right hand: "Is. There. Some. Problem." He grinned, wiggling his fingers in the air. "Four words."

Turman nodded wearily, saying, "You're right." Then he sighed, inhaling deeply, exhaling with, "Listen, you're looking a bit disheveled these days. And I'm just wondering if you might need a break. You know, maybe get some help."

Bing frowned.

Help? Disheveled?

Bing reached to straighten his bow tie, but realized he'd forgotten it at home. So he smoothed a hand through his hair, feeling oil slick his palm. Then he sneered. He sneered with an expression that said, "You don't know what you're talking about."

But that's not what came out of his mouth.

"You're trying to get rid of me, aren't you? You all are, I know it."

Turman recoiled, surprise showing on his face.

"God, man, no," he replied. "That's not what I'm suggesting. I'm thinking about you, as your friend."

"You're my friend?" Bing asked. "You are—?"

"You know I am."

Bing aimed a shaky index finger at him.

"Well, I'm fine, right?"

Then he turned the finger on himself.

"Am I drunk? Have I—have I—did you—is this about Vanderhoof? Has that monster been talking?"

"This isn't about her."

Bing's hands were trembling, his cheeks burning red. He imagined leaping from his chair, flying at Turman's throat, strangling him.

Cocksucker.

"I'm not drunk," Bing said. "Not yet!"

"Didn't say you were—"

"Haven't done anything to anyone. You know I haven't been well, but I'm here for my class, aren't I? Just the medication for my stomach, that's all—it puts a strain on me—but I'm here, Mike. I'm here—"

Turman bent forward, resting a hand on Bing's shoulder. "I know you are," he said, "so please don't be upset. I'm thinking about your health, nothing more. You've looked ragged the last couple of weeks and I'm worried. No one has been talking, okay? This isn't about anything—other than my own concern about you."

Great, Bing thought, the biggest faggot on campus is concerned about me. "Don't worry yourself," he said, forcing a smile.

Turman tightened his grip on Bing's shoulder, flexing his hand: "Just know that if you need time away, whenever, you got it. No problem."

"I appreciate it," Bing said, "except I'm fine, really,"

because he knew this was his last semester. But Turman didn't know yet. No one did. Still, Bing was certain he'd be leaving—and it would be on his own terms, not anyone else's.

"You're positive?"

"Yes."

Then Bing excused himself, practically running from Turman's office. And each person he passed in the hallway, students and faculty, seemed to gaze at him with contempt—or was it amusement?

Fuckers, he thought, each of you—fuckers!

He fled toward the nearest exit, huffing, and sprinted outside, pausing only to catch his breath. It didn't matter that his coat was left behind (his blood felt hot enough, his skin flushed). No, he wouldn't go back—not into that building, not along that hallway, no. Anyway, he needed to be somewhere else, somewhere quiet. He needed to be alone. He needed a drink.

"Fuckers," he wheezed in the chilly afternoon, "fuckers—!"

30.

BING'S THOUGHTS were clearer now, as if the breeze blowing around him, rifling his hair and pushing the leaves along, had somehow billowed through his ears—in one, out the other—removing the clutter that had settled there.

Buzz buzz.

"Another, sir—?"

"No, just the bill, thank you."

"Certainly."

The wine had warmed him thoroughly, so he felt ready to go home and relax. And, Bing decided, he'd give Susan a kiss (she won't expect that). He'd give Pussy a kitty treat (maybe some tuna). Also, he'd call Nick and apologize for the previous night ("If I said or did anything that offended, then I'm truly sorry."); he'd mention the medication and the alcohol, how he'd been unwise mixing the two. Being such an affable young man, Nick would surely understand. There'd be no hard feelings. They'd leave the whole dreadful affair in the past, all of it: disregarding Bing phoning Nick, asking the boy to bring a bottle of wine because the cache of merlot was empty; overlooking that when Nick arrived, paper sack in hand, Bing had greeted him in the study with a hug, saying, "You're my beautiful friend, you know that? You are—"

But not forgetting he still owed Nick for the wine, a cheap red; such a bad vintage, actually, that the boy refused a glass. Or perhaps, as Bing suspected, Nick realized his former professor was so far gone that there'd be no point in joining him: Was I in my robe? Had I showered? Was it difficult standing up (the medication, I swear, making me unstable)?

Bing had settled on the couch, patting the cushion to his right, slurring the words, "Please, sit here, please—"

And Nick obliged.

"You're a wonderful young man—"

"I know, you keep reminding me."

"You really are—"

Of course, the boy figured Bing needed another body nearby—nothing sinister in that. Nothing sinister in resting a hand on Nick's knee (they were friends, like father and son, almost). Then Bing couldn't hold the misery inside any longer. "They're ruining me," he said. He cursed the Trinity, explaining that they were destroying his career with overview classes, compounding the drudgery of life by forcing mindless students on him. "But not you. You're smart, Nick, you're different from them."

The boy was sympathetic, Bing could tell. So sympathetic, in fact, that he rubbed Bing's shoulders and said everything would be okay. Then Nick suggested an evening out sometime, a rendezvous at a beer garden or pub, a place where they could both begin drinking from scratch, no head starts.

"We'll get on the same wavelength then, all right?"

"Sounds good," Bing said. "Sounds grand."

When Nick excused himself and stood, Bing asked for another hug; he climbed from the couch, staggering into the coffee table—and the boy reached for him, keeping Bing on his feet.

Then they embraced.

"Goodnight, be careful."

"You too."

After that Bing remembered Nick at the bottom of the stairs, unlocking the front door, saying, "Goodnight, Mrs. Owen." (Susan must've been in the living room, must've been sitting in the darkness with the television on.)

But now at Eric's, Bing sensed something went wrong there in the study. Except it wasn't his fault. That's what he'd tell Nick: "If I seemed strange last night, it wasn't me—I hope you know that. I'm sorry if I did anything, it's these pills and the wine and I'm rather tired of late."

Friends, right? No hard feelings. Leave it in the past, okay?

"Don't worry," Nick would say.

"Thanks, I knew you'd understand."

So Bing let the wind push the previous night from his memory. Tonight, a quick phone call would put everything in order. No worries. He lifted the bill from the table, checking the tab. Then he felt for his wallet: Where are you? Here? No. Here? No.

Buzz buzz.

"I'm sorry," he told the waiter. "I seem to have left my wallet in my coat."

TONG

31.

"LET'S GIVE it a try, come on. Let's solve the mystery once and for all, ruin it for everyone. Then it'll be your second find here, Tong. And my first. We'll put an end to the Ghost Lights. How about it?"

So it was Tong's assistant who aimed the large telescope at the earth: Kitt, a thirty year old graduate student from the University of Texas. What a plump brunette she was, full of dedication, a great drinker and funny as hell, Tong believed. He was smitten with her, couldn't help himself—though he felt puny in her presence, insignificant, being sixteen years her senior with a round Chinese head and myopic vision (a curse for an astronomer). But Kitt was unattached and didn't mind the long nights at the observatory with him. Sometimes they shared a twelve pack of Miller Lite in his office—sometimes they got so drunk that she let Tong embrace her awkwardly or snuggle his little body against her. In return, she got control of the telescope, she could do whatever she liked. What did it matter, he had already made his great discovery.

Good ol' Kitt, always a hoot when you're getting drunk, Tong thought. We've worked and worked on top of this mountain—now you want to play. So why not?

"Okay, okay—"

The Ghost Lights of Marfa, Texas—those unexplained glowing orbs that appeared almost every evening at the base of the Chinati Mountains, some forty or so miles away. *Ghost lights.* People believed what they wanted to believe. Why not destroy the myth, the tourist attraction, have a little fun?

"We'll put this baby to rest, shall we?"

It would make the newspapers, giving Kitt some needed credit.

OBSERVATORY TELESCOPE EXPLAINS EARTHLY MYSTERY

Of course, they wouldn't be the first to try. Just last month a group of Aggie engineers came searching for the source of the lights, bringing along measuring equipment and telescopes, only to leave three days later in frustration. But they didn't have a 2.1 meter telescope at their disposal, as well as a wide range of state-of-the-art instrumentation for imaging and spectroscopy in the optical and infrared.

Fortunately, Kitt was already a master of earthly investigations. Late one afternoon she had spied on the city of Marfa, spotting cowboys wrangling cattle, teenagers riding in the bed of a pickup. Prairie life. All the comings and goings of a small town. Traffic lights, dogs and horses, men and women. Children running around on a school playground, kids like ants roaming everywhere—and she studied it all as if it were a remote galaxy cluster: "Big sister's watching you—that's right, earthlings, go about your business."

Yet the ghost lights would prove more elusive. Training the telescope on them was the easy part—"Christ almighty, Tong, I got one!"—as was pinpointing the exact location. And Tong (who had never shown interest in the phenomenon, never thought for a second the lights really existed) stepped up to the telescope and immediately saw a distant gleaming ball. He was amazed: the light down below and SN 1999B above, very different things, even if the light looked like a star, and SN 1999B was once a shimmering ball of light. Except there was no SN 1999B anymore, all gone now, just a remnant with a gaseous ring, and too bad, Tong thought, and what a shame it couldn't have been seen like this. Still, it wasn't a ghost, perhaps just an optical illusion, or an elaborate prank. So if he had to accept a mystery at face value, if it was a matter of trusting his myopia, if he had to ponder the reality of a solitary ghost light—"can't fool me, I'm not easily convinced of anything"—then it had to be a hoax. But it should have been a star.

The following morning, when they traveled to the precise spot where the light had materialized, convinced a sign of the source would be readily apparent—possibly tire tracks, at least shoe prints—they found only grass and rocks, scrub brush and dirt.

"Maybe we're pointing those telescopes in the wrong directions," Kitt said, chomping chewing gum as she spoke. "Maybe there's more interesting things going on down here, you know, on the third mall from the sun."

And with the morning light glinting off her dark-brown hair, her mouth making smacking noises with the gum, her ample breasts obvious beneath a tight white T-shirt, Tong was inclined to agree.

NICK

32.

AT HIS table in the library basement, Nick tried composing an embittered poem (a sestina, thirty-nine lines, divided into six stanzas of six lines, ending with a tornada of three lines), one which would accurately express his anger at Bing. But, after some effort, all he could manage was a working title. *Dirty Old Troll.* Then how difficult it was to move his pen, how insurmountable it was to channel his thoughts into stanzas. His memory just wouldn't let him concentrate, so instead he sat with his eyes shut, allowing the previous evening's drama to unfold once again.

"Can't get it out of my head," he'd told Takashi earlier. "It's like a bad movie that won't quit playing."

"Put it on paper," The Shadow suggested. "Make a poem and then burn it or something. Start with the phone call, and take it from there."

Start with the phone call.

Start with Bing's voice on the other end of the line: "Hey, kiddo—got a problem here—"

The man was obviously drunk, his speech somewhat sluggish and garbled ("Like a cassette getting munched by my truck's tape player," was how Nick described it to Takashi). But Nick had little trouble understanding Bing, even if his wording seemed odd.

"Big favors, right? Right. I'm too far gone to go myself—so you'd be a friend and get me a cheap bottle, okay? Could you—would you do that? For me? I'm completely out, right?"

"Sure."

Nick failed to mention that he was exhausted, that the phone was ringing as he'd entered HQ, sweaty and flushed, having returned from a late afternoon jog.

140

"Give me half an hour or so, because I need a shower."

Bing lowered his voice, almost whispering, "Shower here—I can watch," then he burst out laughing, snorting and huffing like a madman.

"I'll pass," Nick replied, vaguely amused by the comment.

"Having you on," Bing cackled, his laughter suddenly ending with a series of harsh coughs.

"But I should've known something was up," Nick later said to Takashi, "especially when I arrived at his house and he greeted me at the door in his robe. But it wasn't just that—his robe was untied, and he was wearing briefs and a white T-shirt. His hair was crazy, and he had a tough time holding the door open for me. Soon as I was inside, he hugged me—this big, sloppy hug, which was freaky considering he was in his underwear. And while I was walking beside him, going upstairs, I swear I got the creepiest feeling."

The overhead light was off in Bing's study, with the only illumination coming from the Frank Lloyd Wright lamp on his desk, shading the room in a dim yellowish hue. The stereo broadcast an easy listening station, and Elton John was busy singing the last verse of "Candle In The Wind" as Nick handed Bing the bottle he'd bought for him.

"Hope it isn't too crappy for you."

"Never," Bing said. Then he showed his appreciation with another hug, placing a palm across the boy's neck, telling him, "You're so good to me, you're wonderful."

That wasn't the worst of it. But, while recounting the matter for Takashi, Nick found some details, the correct order of events, to be elusive. He knew a half-full bottle of merlot was in plain sight on the wet bar (why had Bing lied about having no more wine?). And, naturally, Bing had asked if he wanted a drink.

"Not tonight, thanks."

So Bing invited Nick to join him on the couch for a bit.

"Should've known better, Tak. I was stupid for doing it,

stupid for plopping down so close to him. He said he wanted to talk about stuff because he was lonely and hadn't talked with me for a while—and I guess I felt bad about that."

But Bing didn't engage Nick in conversation. He didn't ask about the boy's poetry, or how his classes were going; rather he went on and on about the Trinity ("Heartless bastards!"). Then he went on and on about Tong ("Lucky bastard! Should've been me, Nick, you know? Should've been me on that mountain, right?"). He couldn't keep his hands off Nick's leg or neck. He repeatedly touched the boy as he spoke, petting his thigh, stroking the hair along the neckline, making butterflies flutter in Nick's stomach.

"You're good to me. You're a good person, not like everyone else."

The thigh. The neckline. Fingertips reaching to fiddle with Nick's earlobe.

"Listen, I better get going."

"No—"

Bing suddenly hunched over, bringing those fingertips to his eyes, covering his face.

"Stay, please—"

For a moment Nick believed the man was weeping, so he patted Bing's back, saying, "Look, you've had a lot to drink. Maybe we can talk tomorrow. We can start drinking together, at the same time. How's that?"

"Yes, yes, of course." Bing's voice didn't sound overcome; he wasn't crying at all, Nick realized, but simply rubbing his eyes. Then he straightened, breathing hard, asking, "Would you massage my shoulders, at least?"

That creepy feeling, those troubled butterflies, raged inside Nick's belly. "Don't really see myself as a masseur," he said.

Bing sighed.

"That's fine, do your best."

Then it was Nick's turn to sigh, doing so twice as he

kneaded Bing's shoulders, offering a half-hearted massage, until finally he said, "Got to go, I'm sorry."

When the boy stood up, Bing clambered after him—but his legs were wobbly; he staggered forward, bumping his shins against the coffee table.

Nick caught him by the elbow.

"Careful, okay?"

"Yes," Bing said, nodding, "yes," then inhaled a labored breath. As they moved together toward the doorway—Nick hoping for a quick escape—Bing began exhaling raggedly through his nostrils, a snotty, grunting burble.

"Get some sleep, all right?"

Bing said he would. Then he insisted on one more hug. ("Before you go, please.")

"I didn't want to," Nick explained to Takashi, "not after all the weirdness, but I did. I let him hug me. And he wouldn't let go. He just held on like he was drowning or something. I tried pulling away—that's when he did it, that's when he grabbed my dick through my jeans. And then it was like he wasn't drunk at all."

Bing's aim was flawless, his grip firm, and he was smiling, even as Nick grimaced and said, "Okay, stop it—"

With one hand squeezing Nick's side, the other pinching the head of the boy's penis, Bing attempted to kiss Nick's throat: "And this is where I get confused, Tak, because everything happened so fast. I shoved him and grabbed his wrist and twisted it—surprised I didn't get my dick twisted off in the process because he had me supremely. And then I spun him around, like I was a cop about to slap handcuffs on him. Next thing I knew, the fucker's arm was behind his back and I was pushing him. And then I let go and he tripped some, ending up near this bookcase, but he didn't fall and that amazed me because he was so wasted."

Then Bing, still smiling, turned and steadied himself by leaning against the bookcase. He lifted a finger, pointing it at Nick, who was glaring at him from the doorway.

143

"Son, promise me one thing—"

"What?"

"Promise me tomorrow you won't think of me as the professor that grabbed your cock."

"We'll see," Nick said, stepping backwards, shaking his head. You're nuts, he thought. You're sick. Then he left, racing down the stairs, skipping every other step. And in the entryway, as he unlocked the front door, Nick glanced sideways into the living room, where the television flickered in darkness, casting a gray luster across Susan (upright in an armchair, hands folded on her lap, as if she were seated at the end of a church pew or at the rear of a crowded bus).

"Goodnight, Mrs. Owen," he said, short of breath.

But she didn't speak, or even turn her head to acknowledge him. Or maybe she didn't have a chance to reply, because Nick was out the door so quickly, sprinting toward his truck, uttering, "What the fuck—? Jesus, Bing—!"

When he arrived at HQ, Nick went straight to the bean bag chair, where he remained for a time, his face tensed, his hands bunching the material of the chair. Finally, he crossed to his bed and stretched out on his back, folding his arms against his chest.

"Are you okay?"

It was The Shadow who spoke, almost unseen behind his computer screen, busily engaged in an AOL chat room, but somehow sensing Stranger's mood. How did he know? Was it the silence? The lack of a greeting, the expected "hi" or "hello" or "howdy," when either entered their room?

For some reason Nick had to laugh. "No," he said, a chuckle rising in his throat, "I'm not okay."

"Really?"

"Really."

Then he told The Shadow everything—the phone call, the wine, the hugs, the shoulder rub, the grope. Takashi listened, leaving his computer as the story evolved; he bent down beside the bed, his brow creasing with concern. Then

Nick propped himself up while finishing the account (not bothered by The Shadow now reaching for him with both arms).

"It's insane," Nick concluded. "The whole thing is fucked."

"Yes, it is," Takashi said, pulling Stranger closer, embracing him. "He's a dirty old troll."

Dirty old troll, Nick thought, I trusted you.

33.

ON THOSE rare occasions when Nick felt ill or depressed, Takashi became War Nurse Dottie (his voice overtaken by a lilting, feminine tone, his mannerisms softened—limp wrists, pursed lips, swishing hips), and Nick, without much say in the matter, became Soldier Tragically Undergoing Muteness, Paralysis, Yearning; in short, S.T.U.M.P.Y.

"Grand ennui, sweety," War Nurse Dottie often said, "or is it worse?"

"Please, Tak, I'm not in the mood—"

"Tak? Who's Tak? Oh my, you're sicker than I imagined. You're delusional, Stumpy. Here, hon', I'll soothe you with some words of wisdom."

"Stop, it's not funny. Make her go away, Tak."

"Well, I'd rather have a bottle in front of me, Stumpy, than a frontal lobotomy."

That usually fixed a grin on Stumpy's sad face.

Or, in less extreme cases, War Nurse Dottie pressed a palm across Stumpy's forehead ("No fever, dear"), checked his pulse ("Well, at least you're still alive"), then announced the only possible remedy for his condition: "Pizza."

"Garlic and mushrooms? No olives?"

"Garlic and mushrooms and fresh tomatoes, dear, and no olives."

"I'm better already."

Of course, there were several instances where War Nurse Dottie could do little for Stumpy's suffering—like last year when Nick had the flu. All the same, she tended him while he sweated and shivered with fever. Or was it The Shadow who did the dirty work? Putting a wastebasket beside Stranger's bed to catch vomit, dabbing a damp hand towel to his forehead and cheeks. But once the fever broke, once Nick's appetite returned, War Nurse Dottie appeared in all her grandeur, holding a student discount coupon as she ordered a large pizza from Domino's. Then she placed a quilt down on the floor, and she and Stumpy (or was it Nick and Takashi?) had a picnic in the middle of HQ, pigging out and drinking Coke. Never mind that Nick hadn't showered for days, or that the room reeked of sickness. Never mind that War Nurse Dottie or The Shadow or Takashi had been exposed to the flu.

"I owe you big time," Nick had said.

"No you don't," Takashi replied. "You'd do the same for me."

"You know it."

"So there you go."

But that's how they were different, Nick knew; if Takashi were ill, he wasn't so positive he'd stick around and take care of him. He wasn't sure he'd know what to do anyway. Plus, he couldn't stand his own vomit, let alone someone else's—and dumping out the wastebasket after each heave, swathing the chest and face with the hand towel, always checking if anything was needed (water, tea, Tylenol?), Nick couldn't imagine himself being so thoughtful or attentive. He hated that about himself. He just wasn't as decent as Takashi; he could never be a war nurse.

Even today, as Nick moped around HQ, The Shadow remained vigilant, keeping Stranger company, cheering him with bad jokes and junk food: a box of Gummi Bears, a bag of licorice-flavored jelly beans—"Question: How many surrealists does it take to screw in a light bulb? Answer: A fish." And when Bing called, leaving a message on the answering machine ("Hi, Nick, it's me. Guess I had a bit much the other night. Don't remember a lot, except I think I owe you for some wine. Give me a call, please"), Takashi erased the message, then switched the machine off.

"From now on ignore him."

"Don't worry," Nick said. "I'll never speak to that freak again."

Takashi tossed Nick his sneakers, saying, "Come on. We're getting out of here. You need some air or something." But Nick shook his head and let the shoes drop.

"Thanks—but no thanks."

"Yeah, bullshit. Let's go."

Nick shrugged ruefully, nudging one of his sneakers with a foot, as if to prove a point. Then an exasperated sigh passed his lips. He stooped over, grabbing up his shoes. "All right," he said, "if it'll make you happy."

The day was warm, hinting of spring's approach, and the quad teemed with short sleeves and students reclining on the grassy lawns—some reading, others resting beneath the clear sky; among them, pale forearms, soon to be tanned, reached for Frisbees or footballs. But Nick and Takashi crossed the quad, paying no attention to their peers; they continued onward, strolling through the stadium parking lot, leaving campus altogether, heading for the Menil Collection. Something about being around all that art and brilliance, Takashi was certain, would put everything in perspective for Nick. How could depression be conceivable when standing before a Van Gogh sketch? What did the desperate acts of an aging professor mean when contemplating such detail, such design? Thin black lines, fashioning curvy trees and wispy leaves. A perfect doodle.

In less than twenty minutes, there they were—gazing at a Robert Rauschenberg retrospective, pondering his White Paintings series, then his Combines (those two-dimensional paintings combined with everyday objects). But at what point did Nick's disposition lighten? When did he forget Bing, if just for an hour? Was it somewhere between Max Ernst and Jasper Johns, while viewing Magritte's *The Memories of a Saint*?

"So how many surrealists does it take to screw in a light bulb?"

"Puffy clouds, blue sky and ocean, encircled by a red curtain."

"That's right."

Afterwards, they wandered to the Rothko Chapel, that octagonal and austere building which housed fourteen of Mark Rothko's huge canvas panels: three triptychs and five single panels, ranging from dark purple to black. For a while they sat inside the somber chapel—where natural light became diffused through the ceiling's skylights—and said nothing; they simply stayed quiet as their eyes adjusted to the subtleties of the stark paintings. But instead of seizing upon an epiphany while studying each Rothko, Nick's mood grew grim.

Fucking bastard. Why'd you do it, Bing?

And it was as if Takashi sensed Nick's anger, because just then he shoved his left knee against Stranger's right knee, knocked his elbow against Stranger's elbow.

"Coffee," War Nurse Dottie whispered. "Lots of coffee, dear."

Nick glanced at her, spotting the pursed lips, the blinking, fawning eyes.

"Yes," Stumpy said, "and pie. Lots of pie."

34.

THE SUN hovered above House of Pies, but its earlier intensity had waned, and inside the diner, seated alone at a corner booth and smoking, Himiko noticed Nick and Takashi coming across the parking lot with their long shadows stalking behind them. They might have seen her too—peering through the window as they moved closer, waving excitedly as they walked toward the entrance—had Takashi not been in the middle of saying, "We should get the hell out of this town. We should take a road trip, or go camping or something."

"Sounds good to me," Nick said. "I'd disappear tomorrow if I could."

"How about Spring Break? Go to the ocean, drink beer, take it easy."

"Perfect, but not the ocean, Tak. Not for Spring Break. Too many jocks. Too many people. Let's head west, drive out into nothing or whatever."

"Sure, to the sticks then," Takashi said, sounding pleased by the idea.

"The sticks," Nick replied. "Nowhere."

"Excellent."

And no sooner did they step into the diner, when Himiko began calling their nicknames, going, "Hey, Stranger, Shadow, hey," in that giggly voice of hers.

"Shit," Nick said, filling with dread.

But Takashi didn't hear him; he was already striding ahead, pointing in Himiko's direction, apparently happy to find her there. So Nick followed, tripping along indolently, irked because he'd wanted a table for just himself and The Shadow, a corner booth where they could eat pie and continue discussing their Spring Break plans. Of course, Himiko wouldn't let that occur. She was busy clearing her notebook, her backpack, and a worn copy of *Plato's Republic* from the tabletop, making room for their arms. Once the pair slipped into the seat opposite her, she feigned an expression of incredible sadness—or was it pity?—saying, "I heard what happened with Professor Owen. I'm really sorry, Nick."

Heard?

"From who?" Nick asked, incredulous, glancing at Takashi, who looked down shamefully. "Oh, man, you told her, Tak? I can't believe it. Now everyone is going to know." He felt like swatting the bill of Takashi's baseball cap, felt like stomping The Shadow's foot beneath the table.

Takashi glared up at Himiko: "You weren't supposed to say anything, big mouth. Remember?"

Himiko made an O with her lips. Then she slapped both hands over her mouth, her cigarette poking precariously between crisscrossed fingers. "Oops," she said through her hands, "I forgot."

Nick shook his head twice, sighing. For a moment he considered rising from the booth and leaving the diner. But instead he stayed put, frowning while Takashi continued glaring at Himiko—she simply shrugged, turning her head to one side and blowing smoke toward the window. When the waitress arrived, Takashi and Nick took turns speaking gravely.

"Coffee."

"Same here, with cream."

"And a slice of orange meringue."

"Same here."

The threesome appeared so gloomy that the waitress asked, "Someone die?"

"No," Nick told her, "not yet."

Then, as the waitress left with their orders, Himiko said, "Don't kill me, Nick. I really won't tell anyone, okay?"

"Yeah, right—"

"I swear."

With her left hand, she dropped her cigarette butt into a glass of water; with her right hand, she crossed her heart.

"I promise. Anyway, it doesn't make you look bad or anything. I mean, it makes Professor Owen look awful and creepy. I mean, he is creepy, you know. I think you should report him."

"I'm not going to do that," Nick said. "He's just a messed up old guy."

"That's no excuse. If you want my opinion—"

"I don't."

"Well, if you want my opinion, you should talk to the school paper. What if he tries that with someone else."

"She's right," Takashi said. "He might've done it before, or he might try it on someone else, someone who isn't like you, Nick. Someone who might let him do it."

"That's not my problem," Nick said. "Look, if he taught small children, sure. But he doesn't. That's it. If someone else gets grabbed by him, they can handle it how they want."

"So you're not mad at him?" Himiko asked.

"Yeah, I'm mad as hell because I trusted him. Believe me, I've thought about going over to his place, knocking on his door, and then popping him in the face. Of course, I'm mad—"

"So am I," Himiko said, folding her arms.

"Me too," Takashi chimed in.

And soon after the pie slices arrived, the steaming white coffee cups, Himiko leaned into the table and spoke pressingly, so that Nick gawked at her, his fork caught between plate and mouth: "You should get him, Nick. You should even the score. That's what I'd do."

"What are you talking about?"

Himiko lifted his orange meringue, tilting the plate at a downward angle near Nick's chin. "Like this," she said. "He deserves this—know what I mean?"

"I agree," Takashi said, forking his slice. "He deserves pie, the pervert. He really does, Nick."

A hard furrow formed on Nick's brow. "No, that's stupid," he said, glancing at Takashi. "That's taking the low road." He glanced back at Himiko. The pie.

"But think about what he did to you. You can't get any lower than that."

Suddenly Nick saw it: Bing spattered in pastry shell, in finely shredded orange peel and meringue.

"Why not, Nick? What's he going to do?"

Nick's furrow smoothed. He took the plate from Himiko, returning it to the table, and then held his fork a few inches from his mouth; one eye was cocked, studying the meringue on the utensil, as if weighing the possibilities.

You've got it coming, Bing. You've had it coming for a long time, perhaps.

TAKASHI

35.

It was like eating, Takashi reasoned. Or shitting—something basic that occasionally needed doing; only afterwards did he hate giving in to what, at the time, seemed so essential. And how thrilling it all was—leaving HQ and Nick's contemplation of revenge, saying he had to get a book at the library, walking across the quad with nervous excitement and a sense of purpose. Then, how vaguely humorous to pass a jogger wearing a faded Tina Turner concert T-shirt that read: What's Love Got To Do With It?

Nothing, he thought. Not a damn thing.

Still, love might blossom from such an encounter between strangers, maybe a great friendship—there was more to understand about each other than just sex. But, in the end, neither of them said much. Takashi met him on the roof of the Engineering Building, with a full moon glowing overhead (*I'm pretty nervous and psyched about doing this*, HotJock80 had written in the HoustonMan4Man AOL chat room, *so when we get together it'd probably be better if we just jumped into it right away, that cool?*).

It was all shadow and moonlight. There was an old couch someone had brought to the roof—that's where HotJock80 was waiting—and even while reclining into the cushions the view below was visible: the quad and sidewalks and oaks and Moss' tomb, midnight joggers, a bicyclist, the lamp posts, the distant stadium parking lot. The campus stretched out as a patchwork of dark parcels.

They sat for a few seconds with the generator hum and the steam rising from within the building. Then they glanced at each other, and HotJock80 said, "Want me to do it first? Or you can? Or at the same time?"

But Takashi wasn't exactly sure about what was being offered.

"At the same time?"

HotJock80 shrugged, looking away. And Takashi wondered if he had missed something important. Then HotJock80 said, "Got a girlfriend?"

"No."

Now he was grinning slyly, telling Takashi, "Mine doesn't swallow. She doesn't like the taste. I really want to try this, okay? I want to—" He stopped and for a moment searched Takashi's face, as if expecting some sign of recognition—then he nodded while scooting closer, saying, "I'll do you first, all right?"

"Okay, if you want—"

Their thighs and legs were touching and Takashi was suddenly frightened. Steam billowed from a nearby vent, got caught by the breeze, and briefly consumed them like fog. He unzipped Takashi's shorts and then slipped a hand through the fly.

It's because she won't swallow for you, Takashi thought. It's because you want to swallow and get swallowed, you want what you want.

The moon was bright and large and it was as though they were high above the earth and somewhere far away. HotJock80 bent, lowering his mouth to Takashi's lap—and Takashi sensed that he was frightened as well (he didn't look like a jock, he looked like he could be anyone). Then Takashi inhaled deeply, breathing in the night air, exhaling slowly as he shut his eyes—and he wanted to go before it was too late, but he was already weakening, gasping, there upon the roof, and was unable to stop himself.

In less than a minute it'd be his turn.

In less than two minutes it would all be done.

In five minutes he was racing up the steps of the dorm, feeling sickened by himself as he approached the lobby doors.

Idiot, he thought. Moron.

Upon returning to HQ, he went straight to the bathroom, his insides now swirling with regret, removed all his clothing as if each article were contaminated—brushed his teeth twice and then entered the shower, eventually turning the bathroom into a sauna while he soaped and soaped and rinsed and soaped beneath a spray of hot water.

And when Nick opened the bathroom door steam engulfed him, bringing a sweat to his forehead as he stood before the toilet, unzipping his pants to piss. "So tell me, Tak," he said, "is it worth it?"

"What?"

"Getting Bing, like Himiko thinks. Does he deserve it?"

Takashi paused to rinse the soap from his face, then he said, "Yeah, Nick, he does. But then I suppose we all do—but some of us just deserve it more than others, you know?"

Nick zipped his pants up, saying, "I guess that's true, sure." He glanced at the green shower curtain, behind which The Shadow was now rinsing the soap from his chest. "Jesus, you're awfully deep tonight—getting all lofty and fancy in there, Tak."

"Maybe you should pie me then."

"That's not a bad idea," joked Nick. "I'll put you on the list."

"I'm not kidding," Takashi said impatiently, but, having just flushed, Nick didn't hear him; instead Stranger heard the toilet burble and slosh, caught the sounds of water sliding through the pipes, and found himself wondering, for no particular reason, why The Shadow had been in the shower for almost an hour.

BING

36.

HOW ARDUOUS it was for Bing to sleep; some nights he didn't—he roamed his upstairs world, Pussy often weaving around his ankles as he went (through the study, outside on the balcony for a bit, back inside, another drink at the wet bar, through the study once more, the balcony), or rested fitfully in his bed, wakeful and bothered, thinking of every soul that had somehow betrayed him, all those rotten people who conspired against his happiness ("Please wither away and die!"). On nights when sleep came, his dreams played as a chaotic swirl of memory-scenes: his childhood (the box kite he flew with his father at the beach), early college years (divers splashing into the Recreational Center swimming pool), the Star Show intermingled with his current life in Houston (the Trinity and Susan seated in the planetarium while a younger Bing explained Dark Matter). When he awoke at dawn, an unspecific dread consumed his gut, huge and impossible, bigger than the body it occupied. So he would pray for escape, chanting it like a mantra—"Let me go, let me go, let me go—" Eventually he'd sit upright, the words becoming a faint murmur passing between his lips. His feet would find the floor, and then he would stand; a minor miracle, he believed.

The days he didn't teach, Bing fetched the newspaper in his robe. The days he taught, he washed his hands and face in the bathroom, usually shaved and combed his hair. Then he dressed before retrieving the newspaper from the front lawn, stepping into the morning air in the same attire— brown slacks, matching tweed coat, white dress shirt, bow tie. Then breakfast with Susan; him shaking the newspaper open while she served. Then off to the university, though on at least two occasions he forgot where his class was held. Once he wandered into Dr. Rosenthal's lecture. Other times, while standing before his students, Bing simply couldn't remember what he was saying. He'd stop in mid-sentence and begin drifting. But he always found his way back, sometimes by asking an unsuspecting pupil, "Have you been paying attention?"

"Yes."

"I see. Well, your vacant expression tells me otherwise. What were we talking about then?"

Yet no one had complained, at least that he was aware of.

"Each class has a collective identity," Bing told Casey. "And this one isn't too dull. I don't hate them as much as I could."

In fact, the kids smiled when Bing entered the lecture hall. Some joked with him, others asked obvious questions that he answered by rote.

"So Earth is exactly where again?"

"In the suburbs of the Milky Way. Twenty-five thousand light years from the core. We are, I suppose, near the center of a galactic halo."

They didn't mind keeping him on track, reminding him where he'd left off at the conclusion of a previous session. As far as teaching went, the Spring students had become his recall, and he never failed to begin a lecture with, "Where were we?"

Still, some days were better than others.

When he slept well, the days were fairly tractable. When he didn't sleep, the days became as scattershot as his dreams—a mess of words, odd scenes, little details that never quite connected. But he was getting better by degrees, that's what Bing suspected. No more medication (the pills were flushed one night). No more merlot (white zinfandel was a lighter intoxicant). And if Nick would only answer the phone, Bing knew, all would be fine. But the boy was never home. Of course, Bing wasn't sure if he was dialing the correct number anymore; the answering machine message had disappeared, the phone just rang and rang and rang. So he tried calling less often, maybe ten times during the work week (once every morning, once every evening). Then strolling across campus, going from his classroom to Eric's Rotisserie, he peered closely at each boy heading his way, half expecting to catch sight of Nick's blue eyes: Are you him? Or you? Sometimes on those sleepless nights, while pacing his study, Bing entertained the notion that Nick never really existed in the first place, that for some reason he'd invented the boy from his own design; to consider Nick as a product, a bad fancy belonging solely to the imagination, Bing almost felt content—then how less troublesome everything seemed, how uncomplicated. Another minor miracle, he told himself.

37.

BING HAD grown bored with drinking at Eric's. Furthermore, he was sick of drinking by himself at home. To make matters worse, wine had lost its flavor. He couldn't seem to enjoy a glass anymore, or savor much of anything—not the morning's scrambled eggs, not the Timmer's Milk Chocolate Bar he purchased from a university vending machine, not even the Sour Tarts a student had left on his podium. Then he began worrying that his taste buds had become damaged. Yet all this bother didn't keep him from sharing a bottle with Damien, who mistook Bing's silence for anger.

"What's wrong?"

"Nothing."

They were sitting at Eric's, lounging at a patio table, and Damien asked more than once, "Are you upset at me for something? Was it something I did?"

"No."

"So what's wrong then?"

Bing lifted his shoulders and let them drop. But Damien wouldn't let him be; he wouldn't shut up: How haggard Bing appeared these days. How sad. How concerned Damien was—his chattiness tinged with melodrama— because Bing hadn't attended Torch Song Thursday in weeks.

"Are you ill? Dying?"

"No."

Then Damien made jokes, whispered asides: "The waiter is cute—I wouldn't mind him waiting on me hand and foot."

"That'd be nice," Bing said, dryly.

"He can serve me anytime, you know?"

"Yes."

Bing didn't want to talk. What could he say? He wanted only to sit in the sunshine and sip the tasteless wine. But Damien droned on and on—"I'm here for you, you know that, and if it's something to do with me you can always tell me. I won't be hurt"—until the words were lost on Bing's ears. "I'd like to think of us as friends, you know. I hate thinking you might be mad at me for some reason. When I see you like this—"

Bing nodded every so often, but heard little. Then he felt like a ghost, hardly present at all, hanging somewhere between there and nothing; a strange floating sensation, where he became immaterial as the wind, and the sunlight, dazzling leaves in nearby oaks, shone right through him and he couldn't perceive the warmth. He was beyond cold, he was transparent and without substance.

The following day was no different. Back at Eric's again, in the afternoon, this time with Casey. But at least Casey wasn't a rambler. Instead they sat quietly together at the same patio table, nursing their drinks, watching students stroll past on the sidewalk. And Bing was entertaining the idea of escaping Moss, of finding Tong in West Texas and never returning to Houston.

Then, as if on cue, Casey said, "Have you considered leaving? I mean, you just aren't happy, man. Is it worth staying?"

It seemed his colleague had read his mind—and that scared Bing: What else do you know? Is my loneliness also so apparent?

Or perhaps Casey was of a like disposition, and now he was revealing this fact.

Perhaps, Bing thought, you're drifting as well, just not yet as far from the shore.

"No," Bing finally said, "it isn't worth it to stay. But where to go, Casey? I can't leave Susan, you know—she needs me—she's settled here."

Bing could tell Casey understood by the way his head

inclined beneath the canopy of shade: "Of course," he said, then reached across the table, taking hold of Bing's wrist, his fingertips pressing softly. "Maybe we should quit this. You're drinking yourself away. I'm afraid I am too. What do you think?"

"I'm too old to quit," Bing replied. "I don't think I'm strong enough, actually."

"Bing—" Casey started, but didn't continue. His hand then slipped from Bing's wrist, retreating slowly over the tabletop. When Bing looked into his face, he saw an aghast expression, the eyes of a man who'd suddenly met a ghost. And as Bing lifted the glass to his lips, he felt lighter than air.

38.

WHILE WALKING across campus at dusk, Bing beheld oaks throwing wide shadows against red-brick walls. He stepped among the angled brightness of the sun's diminishing light, inhaling the earthen and woodsy aroma enriching Moss (as if dusk carried its own unique scent). Then how tranquil this world felt, how loose and fluent. No worries, he thought. "No worries," he told himself.

He recalled what his mother said when he was a child (for even then his moods were ungovernable, and sadness often weighed heavy): "This too shall pass." So there in the evening—with sunlight hitting his neck, the birds twittering in the branches, and spring making itself known—Bing's psyche unburdened. Forget the two bottles of white zinfandel he'd shared with Casey, or how dour he'd been at Eric's. Forget his mercurial health and the suspect medication and all that sordid business involving others.

"No worries."

Because spring was the season of renewal, and, Bing now believed, he too would be allowed such invigoration—something fresh in his life, a change, a beginning. And what had Tong written last week in an email? What had the message concluded with?: *At last, I'm happy to report, we're ready to begin gathering solar neutrino data. Though I wish you were here, friend. You'd make a grand addition to the team.*

Tong, Bing had thought, I wish I was there collecting data, and I wish you were here struggling with the Trinity, with Nick—with my wife.

"This too shall pass."

That's what he'd told Susan while she recovered in the hospital. He sat beside her bed for days, squeezing her hand, and although she couldn't speak or hear the words, he repeated them again and again, "This too shall pass. Soon you'll be right as rain, right?"

No worries.

So sauntering toward Herbert R. Moss' huge statue (that austere visage leveling the quad with a thousand-yard stare), Bing inhaled the evening, relishing the university's serenity, the mostly barren campus—where only a smattering of students roved about; some heading to the library with backpacks, others crossing his path. He began whistling, blowing a song for no one save himself. A tune from childhood—"I'm Gettin' Sentimental Over You"— which seemed perfect at dusk. Perfect for the golden light and shadows transforming the footpaths and walkways, the dark and near-white contrasting amongst the grass. Perfect for the few young faces that swam toward him.

But who's this?

Coming his way, an Asian girl, apparently giggling and waving with recognition (though Bing couldn't return her enthusiastic greeting; he couldn't place her, wasn't sure he'd ever seen her before). Then they were face to face, paused in front of Moss' tomb, and she shook his hand, saying, "Hello, how are you—?"

"Very good, I suppose. Yourself?"

"Super, thanks for asking—"

But there was something manic about her (the manner in which she clutched his hand so firmly, her brown eyes darting from side to side). She couldn't look directly at him, and he suspected impaired vision: "Possibly you've mistaken me for someone else."

"Professor Owen, right?"

"Yes—"

"Excellent!"

The very instant Bing began to ask if she was in his class, he caught sight of Nick; the boy materializing, it seemed, from nowhere, charging forward with a pastry shell held in the flat of his palm. Suddenly Bing couldn't talk; his voice faltered, a faint hiss passed between his lips. But it wasn't until the girl jumped aside, until the first pie had hit him full on, that Bing realized an ambush was underway. Then he was blind (was it cool vanilla cream obscuring his sight?), his nostrils plugged by filling (the scent of lemon— or orange?), his mouth parting (how sweet and tangy!). The second pie struck him from behind—meringue slapped against the back of his skull, chocolate filling squished down into his collar—so deliberately and forcefully that he stumbled, tripping over his own feet. Then he toppled, groping senselessly as he went, crashing to the path as if a bullet had just torn through his brain. And how aberrant it was to hear Nick yell, "Let's go! Come on!" How singular it was to be sprawled on the ground, the sweetness of dessert on his tongue, and hear footsteps running away. How strange to be that blind and helpless near Moss' shrine, lacking any will to stand and wipe the mess from his head— remaining inert for a while, panting like an animal, and listening as the birds warbled in the oaks.

NICK

39.

GOODBYE, MOSS. Goodbye, HQ. Adios, Bing.

On the third day of their spring break, Stranger and The Shadow gathered their respective sleeping bags, deodorants, toothbrushes, as well as a change of socks and boxers and T-shirts, stuffing all except the sleeping bags into Takashi's backpack (along with Nick's poetry notebook and Takashi's sketchpad). They made a hasty late-night departure from Moss, leaving a solitary Post-It note on the door of HQ that read: <u>GONE JACKALOPE HUNTING IN MARFA!</u>

And while Nick understood it was foolhardy taking his truck beyond the city limits—dumber still attempting a journey deep into West Texas, traveling approximately 1,200 miles round-trip with a vehicle that barely managed grocery store excursions—both he and Takashi knew an entire break spent on campus would be monotonous. But they debated the risk of heading west for days until, finally, Nick said, "Screw it. Let's just go. At worse—if the truck dies—then at least we'll have some adventure."

"At least," Takashi replied, grinning. "At worse, I think, we die too."

"True, but how bad could that be, really?"

Takashi cocked an eyebrow. He pictured them trudging across bleak terrain with cracked and bleeding lips, searching for a watering hole or any sign of civilization as the sun charred their skin. "I guess pretty bad," he said. "We better get Carmex and bottled water if we go."

"And Doritos."

"And smokes."

That was how it went. One moment they were playing Uno on the floor of HQ, discussing the practicality of going, and several minutes later they were throwing clothes into a backpack. In less than an hour, Operation Emancipation was underway—and soon all that remained of Houston was a faint glow in the rearview, a murky pinkish hue rising behind a scar of darkness.

"Where we're going," Stranger told The Shadow, "the stars are brighter than streetlights." Where we're headed, he wanted to say, I once hated more than any place on earth.

"Well, when you get tired, let me know," Takashi said, shaking a cigarette from a new pack. "I can take over whenever. I'm wide awake."

Though before reaching San Antonio, Takashi had fallen asleep, his body slumped against the passenger door, his head resting near the window. So Nick continued onward without The Shadow's company, stopping every sixty or seventy miles to add oil and check the radiator level. With AM talk radio providing interesting entertainment (Art Bell taking phone calls regarding UFO sightings in New Mexico and cattle mutilations in Arizona), a 20-ounce Pepsi in one hand, a large bag of Doritos on the seat between himself and Takashi, Nick was far from flagging; not while his truck kept rolling forward, and the headlights seemingly forged the highway's path—not while traveling at night offered more comfort than sleep.

But weariness caught him at dawn, when the sun rose orange and red above the hill country, and the AM station frequency began fading in and out; the signal competing against a Mexican station broadcasting somewhere beyond Del Rio (the morning farm report eventually losing to Tejano music). Near Junction, where the hill country sloped into the scrub and open spaces of West Texas, The Shadow stirred, blinking awake and sitting upright in the seat with a foul yawn, a hand dipping absently into the Doritos bag.

"Where are we," Takashi asked.

"More than halfway, I think. Yeah, I know we're more than halfway—"

Fatigue lifted from Nick's throat, manifesting as a hoarse grumble—and in the light of day, The Shadow thought Stranger's face looked pasty and unhealthy (bloodshot eyes roamed below drooping lids, the beginnings of a stubble dotted the chin), so Takashi insisted on driving, saying, "You're wrecked. Time for bed."

"You're right," Nick said, knowing he was ready for sleep, was ready to lean his body into the passenger door and let the tires humming on asphalt carry him away.

Once Takashi was settled behind the steering wheel—after they'd stopped on the shoulder to urinate, add oil, switch places—he told Nick, "Don't worry, I'll get us there. You just rest easy." Then every so often, while Nick napped, he became aware of Takashi gently patting his leg, of fingers brushing along his jeans, as if to assure him that all was going well in the driver's seat.

But it was a disjointed slumber, punctuated by the sounds of Takashi fiddling with the tuner dial, the Doritos bag crackling, the road map crumpling, or sometimes The Shadow's voice joining a Tejano hitmaker's chanting ("Tu sexy tu, tu sexy tu—"). And Nick faded in and out like those radio stations, waking occasionally to glimpse the lunar countryside sliding past in the flat midday light. Then dreams came, pushing him ahead, bringing him to Marfa hours before actually arriving there—to the old house, where his mother hung damp and squirming kittens on the clothes line; to the halls of his high school, where he wandered naked and unseen among children with buckets covering their heads.

40.

STRANGER, HAVING climbed into the driver's seat somewhere on the outskirts of Marfa, now assumed the role of
mobile tour guide—cruising leisurely around and through
his former hometown, which, compared with the movement
and sprawl of Houston, seemed like a throwback to a more
stated, less complicated era. But the town and its history,
Nick told The Shadow, was not without importance or
unique grain; for once James Dean, Rock Hudson, and
Elizabeth Taylor slept in the Spanish-style El Paisano Hotel
while filming *Giant* in 1955—then there was the artist
Donald Judd, who had left New York in the early '70s,
bringing his singular vision (the creation of permanent
installations for public viewing) and a large collection of
modern art along with him. And in that region of West
Texas, where people were few and the land remained uncor-
rupted by development (rangeland mixed with desert scrub
and riverbeds, mountains cracked the horizon in each direction), mystery lights existed some nine miles from Marfa,
appearing almost nightly since 1883: small, ethereal orbs
glowing and floating at the base of the Chinati Mountains;
a phenomenon that continually defied any explanation.

"You know though, nothing changes much here," said
Nick. Even Marfa High School remained as it had, though
he failed to recognize the boys playing basketball on the
outside court, or the P.E. girls jogging around the track
field. Same but different, he thought. Then the house where
he had lived—that box-like pre-fab on the edge of town—it
too was familiar and transitory; the roof was still in disrepair, the screen door ragged, but someone had hung a tire
swing from the oak in the front yard, toys littered the lawn,
and a yellow Camaro was parked in the spot once reserved
for his stepfather's Suburban.

How long had it been? Almost two years?

Same but different: He had lived there, had sweated through puberty on the track beside the football field, had peered through a telescope while standing in the yard of the old house; then upon returning—aware of each street name, anticipating every bump in the road—Nick marveled at the lack of connection. But acting as tour guide, if only for a day, he soon realized that what had felt provincial and confining as a teenager unexpectedly seemed curious and rich as an adult. "Like looking at an ant farm," he told Takashi later that afternoon, "instead of being stuck inside it."

They were now sitting amongst scrub brush on private property, near the ruins of the Big House from *Giant*, where several large wood beams jutted skyward like telephone poles, the only standing remnants of the set.

Takashi laughed. "I think it'd be easy to think you're an ant way out here," he said, glancing up from his sketchpad, taking in a view which afforded a grand fifty mile panorama, a sublime expanse of nothingness.

"Ninety percent sky," Nick said, opening his poetry notebook, "ten percent earth."

They had parked the truck along the shoulder of Highway 90, crawled between the top and bottom wires of a fence, and hiked to the ruins with the idea of getting some work done. But for a while it was hard focusing—"Can you imagine James Dean and Rock Hudson being right here?"—so they sat quietly in the brush, respective folios on their laps, breathing the spring air, savoring the countryside. Then, as if stirred by the sudden breeze that trembled the scrub, Takashi started sketching—his pencil moving quickly, his eyes going repeatedly from the pad to Nick. Stranger was already writing, oblivious to The Shadow's glances as he began a first stanza, something that had been forming in his mind since driving past Marfa High School.

The boy ran for four years
in his white tennis shoes, his gray shorts,
hoping to go as far away
as his strong legs and wide feet
would carry him—
shuffling on, not stopping
for rest or remembrance;
shutting his eyes from time to time
biting his bottom lip, so certain
he would never return home,
would keep moving onward
for four years
around and around
the only paved track in town.

Then as the afternoon waned—the breeze increasing in strength, the sun heading for the horizon—they stood and paused to watch the diminishing sunlight cast their shadows across the ruins, slowly angling their forms up a wood beam and out into the brush—until their shapes finally became indistinguishable. In the lingering light before nightfall, Takashi opened his pad, showing Nick one of the sketches he'd made: Stranger detailed in pencil, gazing down thoughtfully at his notebook; his legs crossed amongst tall growing scrub, his hair ruffled by the breeze, the stubble on his chin embellished and exaggerated from the thickness of lead. And although Nick immediately recognized himself, he didn't like how somber and thin his face appeared, or how Takashi had captured the dark circles beneath his eyes, revealing what little sleep he'd had in the last twenty-four hours.

I'm as scrubby as those brush weeds, Nick thought. "Pretty hyper real," he said, smiling. "But I look homeless and starving."

"You are," Takashi said, flipping the pad shut. "So am I."

Then The Shadow threw an arm around Stranger, and

the pair turned and started toward the truck while making plans for the evening—hamburgers and home fries and Cherry Cokes at the local Dairy Mart. Then mystery lights. Then sleep.

41.

AT THE Mystery Lights viewing area, some ten miles from Marfa, the truck had had enough—but, as far as Nick and Takashi were concerned, she couldn't have picked a more appropriate spot for the battery to expire. With the tank half full, oil level good, it seemed she just got tired of moving (a low keen rumbled from the engine when Nick tried the ignition, as if protesting, "Christ, I'm tired, give me a break!"). So the decision of where to camp was made by chance; they'd rough the viewing area for the night, nesting in the truck bed, eventually falling asleep beneath a canopy of stars (their stomachs well sated from a Dairy Mart gorgefest). What a great place to be after dusk, Nick thought, sitting on the tailgate with The Shadow, waiting for ghost lights—those distant glowing spooks, somewhat like massive cotton balls.

Takashi watched expectantly, scanning the base of the Chinati Mountains, squinting.

"Is that one?"

"Nope."

"Think I saw one."

"Nope."

Though soon enough two lights materialized, bobbing and weaving, dimming in and out. "Holy shit," Takashi said, nudging Nick excitedly. And Stranger, having seen the lights more times than he could remember, was charmed instead by The Shadow's reaction (Takashi cupping a hand across his mouth, giggling maniacally like Himiko). So Nick mentioned his mother's story—how she claimed several lights once flew down the side of the mountain, heading directly toward her car, stopping near the hood: "I could swear they were alive," she said, "because they shot right up to the windshield like curious critters at a wildlife park—then zoomed on about their business!" Nick never believed her, but he always wanted the story to be true. Still, he told Takashi, the lights were a tangible mystery—not like Loch Ness, or Bigfoot, or UFOs; those oddities that only a few people encountered. The Mystery Lights were for everyone. On most clear nights they recurred, keeping just far enough away so that a decent look was impossible.

"Amazing," Takashi said. "Should've brought a camera."

"It'd be too dark anyway."

"That's true."

The lights played for almost an hour—sometimes dancing in pairs then dimming, sometimes glimmering alone—before disappearing altogether. Then it was Nick and Takashi's turn to fade. They unrolled their sleeping bags in the truck bed, removed their shoes, and crawled between the warm lining. But the night had gradually grown chilly, the coldness of it creeping into the bags, and their breaths soon shuddered from them like smoke.

"God, it's freezing—"

"I know—"

So Takashi suggested zipping the sleeping bags together. "We'll get more body heat going."

"Good idea—"

Afterwards they cozied themselves within one huge sleeping bag, shoulders touching, and stared skyward. Then how beautiful the heavens appeared above them, how radiant and pure; Nick had almost forgotten.

"That's why McDonald Observatory got built here, way up on the Davis Mountains. No city lights, no pollution, no nothing."

Stranger pointed at a few stars, directing The Shadow to the first constellation his stepfather had shown him (six years earlier, man and stepson standing behind a cheap store-bought telescope, studying the Little Dipper).

"Hey, Nick," Takashi said, "where's your real dad? You never say."

The inquiry came unexpectedly, interrupting Nick in mid-sentence (he'd been talking about the Little Dipper, explaining how the four stars in the bowl were almost exactly second, third, fourth, and fifth magnitude). For a moment he didn't respond, thinking instead about The Shadow's own father, Dr. Shimura, who had died of lung cancer when Takashi was ten. Nick's father, however, was a different story: He was six months old when the man was killed; that's what he told The Shadow, adding that his mother had given him two photographs (a blurry black-and-white picture of his father brandishing a chain saw, the other—a color snapshot—showing his father standing at the edge of the Grand Canyon, arms outstretched), and, aside from a ponytail and thick reddish mustache, his resemblance to the man was uncanny.

"Was he nice?"

"I guess." But all Nick really knew about his father was that he liked Coors and fly-fishing—and that one rainy evening, three days following his twenty-second birthday, he slid his Harley-Davidson into the wheels of an oncoming semi-truck: "My mother never talked much about him—I never asked much about him. I grew up knowing her boyfriends mostly—the banker from Dallas, the vet with a limp, the lobbyist guy from Austin. Then my stepfather. I suppose he arrived when I was about nine—she married him not long after that—that's when we went to Arizona to live for a while."

"You miss him?"

"Who? My father?"

"Yeah—"

Nick had to think.

"I don't know. How could I—?"

Takashi turned on his side, saying, "I miss mine, I miss him all the time."

Nick could smell The Shadow's breath—strangely pleasing aftertastes, flavored Coke and cigarettes—and feel the heat of it spread across his chin. There in the bright nighttime he could almost make out The Shadow's face— brown eyes gazing intently, white teeth shining between dark lips. He reached out, resting a palm against Takashi's neck. Then Nick kissed him on the forehead, surprising himself. Takashi exhaled deeply while bringing cold hands to Nick's chest.

"I love you," The Shadow said, his voice abstracted and wavering.

"I know," Stranger whispered, before putting his tongue in Takashi's mouth and pulling him closer.

42.

THE HIGHWAY patrolman's name tag simply read: HAYWOOD. He looked like a Haywood too, Nick thought, with those aviator sunglasses and crewcut, that sunburned forehead and squarish jawline. Yet it was the patrolman's voice, very Texan, gruff and sharp at once, which unnerved Stranger: "You'll be needing to come out of there right now!"

The cold night had passed. Beyond the viewing area parking lot the clouds reddened just above the Chinati Mountains, and the dawn sunlight brought heat. But hours earlier the temperature had dipped to almost freezing—so Nick and Takashi cuddled together (The Shadow's back pressed snugly against Stranger's chest, their legs intertwined). Sometime during the night, the pair enclosed themselves completely within the joined sleeping bags, yanking the drawstrings above their heads and bunching the top closed. "Our cocoon," Takashi said wearily, a hand lingering in the cup of Nick's armpit. Then they slept, shifting rarely, skin always touching skin. And they would've remained like that well into the morning if not for the firm shake from outside, jostling Nick's shoulder, and that harsh voice saying, "You'll be needing to come out of there right now!"

Takashi stirred, whispering at Stranger, "Who is it?"

"Come on now, out—!"

Nick nervously squeezed his head through the opening, his sight overwhelmed for a moment by the brightness— then Haywood became apparent, standing beside the truck bed, no doubt fixing Stranger with a hard stare from behind his sunglasses, taking in a puffy face and blinking eyes, a shock of sandy hair. Then Takashi's head emerged, appearing alongside Nick's confused expression, and to the patrolman the pair looked like some grotesque two-headed larva, uncomfortably occupying the same pupa.

"Mornin'."

"Morning."

When Nick saw the name tag, black shirt and badge—the dark glasses, the rectilinear lips—his stomach knotted with fear; he imagined what the patrolman might think—that young men sharing sleeping bags were probably more than friends. But Haywood's stoicism collapsed with a smirk: "Keeping yourselves warm?"

"Yeah," Nick replied, reaching blindly in the bag for his T-shirt. "We didn't know it'd get freezing."

The patrolman nodded. "College students?" he asked.

"Yes sir," Nick replied. "From Houston. On Spring Break."

"That right," Haywood said, fanning his fingers out, tips against the ledge of the bed. His head moved a bit; Nick knew that he was now studying The Shadow, perhaps wondering when he last encountered an Asian boy near Marfa, especially one who looked so disheveled and tired. "Well," he said, "there's no overnight camping allowed here."

Nick had his T-shirt around his neck. "Wasn't really our plan," he said, squirming around inside the bag, tugging his arms into the sleeves. "My battery went dead."

The patrolman nodded again, slowly. "I see," he said. "Get the hood popped, let's jump it."

Nick scooted himself from the bag and climbed over the ledge of the bed, landing on gravel that stabbed at his bare feet. Then he went into the cab, popped the hood, and—after the patrolman had pulled his car closer, once Haywood had deftly applied the cables to both vehicles—tried cranking up his truck, which, following two near starts, rumbled to life. By then Takashi had dressed; he'd already unzipped, rolled up, and tied the sleeping bags, pushed the tailgate shut, and—having lit a cigarette as he walked several yards away—was staring thoughtfully at where the ghost lights had flitted about. But once the truck rattled awake, momentarily spewing thick exhaust from the tail pipe, he about-faced, flicking his cigarette butt, and trudged back. Approaching the truck, where Haywood now leaned into the driver's door, his chin practically on Stranger's shoulder, Takashi expected to hear the patrolmen's stern voice telling Nick, "Well, I'll just give you a warning this time around, just don't go camping out this way again." Or, "You better get going now, okay?" But instead Haywood said, "You boys be careful getting home."

"We will," Nick said, shaking the patrolman's hand. "Thanks for the help."

"No problem."

Then Haywood ambled to his patrol car, giving the pair a wave before slipping behind the wheel. When Takashi entered the cab, he ran a hand through his morning hair, saying, "That was scary," as if he and Nick, reeking of something taboo and shameful, had narrowly avoided capture.

"Yeah," said Nick, sighing, "but at least he got us running."

They motored through Marfa a final time, Stranger and The Shadow, saying little to one another as the return journey commenced. And if the pair had been filled with excitement while departing Houston (the sense of adventure saturating their conversation), they headed back under a malaise which was punctuated only by radio music, breaks for gas and oil, and the switching of places. Still, Nick discerned what was hanging between himself and The Shadow (a kiss, a confession of love, then another kiss—that connection suddenly obliterated by the grumbling voice of a highway patrolman), but Nick didn't want to talk about it. Tak, you don't either, he thought. You'd rather not know how I feel about everything—because I'm not sure myself.

Eventually the radio offered nothing more than static. And when reaching the desolation between Ozona and

Sonora—where a dull midday light muted the landscape, accentuating the listlessness that existed in the truck—Nick began yawning, his involuntary intakes of breath spreading to Takashi. So they exited at a rest area, parking alongside a semi hauling a trailer loaded with cattle, the smell of cow shit sneaking into the cab as they napped. Then how unusual it was—there in West Texas, among open prairie and cattle—for Nick to dream of Bing, to find himself in Houston again and sitting on the man's couch ("Delightful," Bing was saying, pouring wine into Nick's glass. "You are delightful, my friend!"); they were laughing, genuinely happy about something. How extraordinary coming awake from that dream—somewhat disoriented, needing to urinate—and, after crossing the rest area parking lot, noticing an empty wine bottle in the trash can outside the Men's toilets: Poor Bing, Nick thought. Poor stupid Bing.

Then Stranger couldn't get the man from his mind. For the first time, he felt real regret about ambushing him—this as he drove from the rest area, as the truck puttered onto the highway, as Takashi stared through the windshield and seemed lost in his own ruminations.

Stupid drunk idiot—

Because Bing had been a friend of sorts—at the very least an ally—but he couldn't escape representing all those interloping, rigid, self-important adults (how wonderful it was that at Moss such people were often singled out by The Pi Crusters). And Nick, who trusted so few people—whose dislike of convention had always kept him moving forward, that is, never allowing him the true pleasure of belonging to anyone or anyplace—had proven he was nobody's fool, especially not Bing's fool (a well-aimed lemon meringue had made that point). But then again, he wondered, was it worth humiliating the man? And which betrayal was crueler—a pie in the face or a pathetic grope? Was Bing's groping any more inexplicable than the yearning for a best friend, than the need to bring one's self closer to someone dear—for whatever reason? No, he concluded, not at all.

Now with Marfa behind him, Houston ahead, Nick was at ease while driving in the late afternoon. He was resigned to forgiving Bing, and knew making his own amends would probably be helpful. "Before you shake a finger or strike at someone," he remembered his mother telling him as a boy, "you best take a good look in the mirror—you probably could use a slapping from yourself." As the declining sun lit the spring sky and the countryside was a flat dirt ocean of orange, his thoughts roamed wildly, sending him once more to the previous evening. So he observed the beginnings of sunset, and noted the shifting of colors across the land— how bright orange turned rusty, the scrub brush appearing like small fires on either side of the asphalt; then he found himself among the curious moments that only yesterday— he understood now—had pushed him into new territory. Again he sensed the coldness that settled over the viewing area, touching all that had occurred: the ghost lights and the stars; the slow turning of constellations; the urge to taste The Shadow's mouth; the strange force that had drawn their bodies together. Then, finally, Nick thought of love and how, when he had held Takashi within the bag, the desire to never let go had felt mysterious and unique, as puzzling and elusive as those glowing balls that hovered just after dusk. And the one image he recalled clearly, there on the highway, was of those mystifying lights, aglow in the evening, whose reason or source had eluded even science; a marvel more incomprehensible than the confounding passion that surfaced with a kiss, or than a young man finding nothing unusual in the existence of ghost lights.

Nick fiddled the radio dial, absently searching for any station that could replace the low hiss of static (almost four hours without music or talk programs, the airwaves seemingly dead during the day). The sun was slipping under the horizon, bathing the highway and surrounding scenery in red—and he watched as the earth grew darker from minute to minute, as if somehow absorbing itself in degrees and gradually becoming a vacuum. The mesquite trees and prickly pears, most consumed by shadows, contrasted sharply amongst the last burning patches of terrain. Further on, the hill country loomed, already swallowed in night. The rising shadow now inside the truck filled the floorboards and Stranger's lap; the eastern horizon seen beyond the windshield had diminished, turning to a black-blue sweep mixed with the soft flickering of starlight.

Suddenly, as Nick was about to give up on the radio, music crackled through the speakers; the final verse of Buddy Holly's "Learning The Game" broadcasting faintly from some podunk station, followed immediately by Santo and Johnny's instrumental "Sleepwalk." The song ebbed and then returned, coming in varying fluctuations which enlivened the darkness. That lazy guitar didn't so much mask the grating drone of wheels as calm it and push it far away. And Nick listened, daring to close his eyes briefly on that straight highway; then opening them again, he found himself buried in twilight with the truck's headlights dimly navigating the road. The day was finished. He glanced at Takashi, wanting just then to tell him something important, to say the words he knew The Shadow wished to hear. But Takashi had fallen asleep—his body sagging into the passenger door, his right cheek pressed against the window—so Nick reached for his pliant hand instead, placing it in a palm, holding it for a while as he drove them home.

MARC

43.

THERE WERE afternoons in the country, evenings upon a blanket in the woods. So it wasn't exactly like now—two men marching indignantly together, holding hands if they chose, kissing in public. No, it was more covert then, less open for most. Never was a relationship explicit, unless it was behind closed doors, somewhere discreet, or far from any cities (like Winston and Julia in Orwell's *1984*, Marc had imagined): a meadow, a grassy field where the only observers would be birds and insects.

He rested his head on Bing's stomach. He stared upward at the tall spruces and the clouds and the blue sky and the faint thumbnail moon and felt Bing's skin on his neck, warm and fuzzy, like a flimsy pillow without a case, rising and falling, lungs working, like an object meant solely for his well-being, a safeguard. Then he'd stare at Bing's embracing arm, draped across his chest; not so much dormant, as the fingers were continually traveling, exploring, gliding—and when those fingers reached Marc's armpit they'd begin tickling, moving frenetically, almost like they did while unbuttoning Marc's shirt or pants. Then he and Bing would be laughing, wrestling, rolling about on the blanket, and Marc knew it wasn't just a fleeting affair— a married man and a college student—it was much more than that, something unequaled and momentous.

It was more than how their bodies touched or even the way Bing's lips would part so Marc's skin could be savored. It was the cabalism of their need, their occult desire opposing a greater contempt, and it was that which couldn't easily be placed amongst the everyday indiscretions happening elsewhere—the little scandals involving secretaries, the broken homes. Marc believed that Bing might think the same, that such love was like the shadows weaving through and around the dying grass; it was like the space surrounding the stars.

"It's beautiful here."

"Yes, it is."

"I don't want to leave."

Head on Bing's stomach; they could've traded off: Bing could've rested his neck against Marc's belly, he wouldn't have minded. That was how Marc liked it, so why ruin a good thing, why disrupt the moment, why say, "But we should be going—it's getting late, I should get home, okay?"

So they stood and began dressing, and Marc would soon experience the vague, muted, bubble-in-the-gut sensation of jealousy. It never came right away. First the socks had to be donned and the blanket folded and the picnic basket packed and the wads of implicating toilet paper buried in a small hole. But once they were on the highway the jealousy would stir like bile, until finally anger would take over and he'd struggle to hold it in.

How can she mean anything to you?

Still, Marc never erupted, never threw a fit (Bing was unaware of any turmoil, whistling as cool air sailed through the open side windows); he never hit the dashboard and exclaimed, "I'm tired of this, it's either me or her, you can't have us both!" Instead he remained calm, at least on the surface, for no other reason than sympathy—Bing's wife was a damaged woman. Because she needed him, Bing had said, she couldn't survive without him—so he would always return to her or feel inclined to be near her, and when he entered their house she'd be there—and Marc would be somewhere else.

But the jealousy and anger always disappeared as they kissed goodnight, and though Marc knew there would be other afternoons and other drives into the country, he wondered how long it could possibly last. When someone has a life with a person, it's impossible to have a life with another. Then unlocking his apartment door, he thought: It's all right, no use worrying about the future while the present is fine—and maybe all is for the best, just as it should be and nothing more. Afternoon picnics and a blanket with me, a dark and quiet home with her.

He figured Bing would've been grateful that his lover tolerated the arrangement for his wife's welfare. So he never complained, never said a word. But perhaps Bing wouldn't have cared, perhaps he'd already resolved the affair in his mind, perhaps he even preferred the way it was, Marc waiting there on the sidelines like some pleasing distraction—and perhaps the only reason he wanted to go home was because he really favored Susan after all.

BING

44.

ON HIS first night in the hospital, Bing shifted restlessly beneath the sheets, wishing a more dramatic and tragic near-death experience had brought him there, like a mysterious push down a long staircase. If it had only been Nick's vicious pie in the face ("You'd be sorry then, kid")—or a poisoned glass of wine served at Eric's; if it had been a gunshot wound from a sniper—or a rope around the neck (the idea of which had grown more appealing in the days following Spring Break); if it had just been the Trinity somehow ("You try and you fail to do me in, ha!")—instead of cholesterol plaque, abnormal heart rhythm, a blood clot obstructing a coronary artery. Ultimately though, Bing wanted to believe it was really laughter that almost put him under. A terrible joke, he thought. My heart couldn't take the telling of it.

"Well, Bing, I've got a pretty tasteless story for you today."

"By all means, let's hear it—!"

"Okay, there's this boy—he's walking along the sidewalk—"

He didn't fault Tong; the man was attempting to cheer him, was doing his best to let Bing know he had at least one solid ally, a buddy. And was the depression so apparent during recent phone conversations ("Nothing has gone right this school year, not a damn thing! Just not happy, Tong. I'm so muddled and lonely, completely pointless")? Yet Tong had become a real sweetheart, calling three times a week, keeping the banter humorous and interesting, even sending a framed photograph of his glorious supernova's remains encircled by a gaseous ring (the gift promptly getting hung on a wall in the office alcove); such thoughtfulness lessened the gloom somewhat, to the point where Bing waited expectantly for his phone calls.

Still, that last damn joke, how awful it was—and funny too (something about a boy finding a welder's mask on the sidewalk and the old pedophile who lures the youngster into his car, the joke concluding with the small victim saying, "To be honest, sir, I gotta tell ya—I'm not really a welder"). Tong had barely spoken the punch line before cracking up. Nervous laughter rose from Bing, accompanied by a pressure in his chest—heartburn perhaps, indigestion?—then a sudden heavy sweat that wetted his forehead. But he couldn't stop laughing, neither could Tong; the two roared and coughed and snorted hysterically like madmen. So much laughter that Bing's jaw ached, and the arm holding the receiver surged with pain.

What a terrible joke!

His back hurt—his breath went, reducing the laughter to troubled gasps—and for a moment Bing felt nauseous.

"Christ—"

What a miserable and horrible joke, making him so tired, bringing him down to the floor of his study—where the phone dropped from his hand, where he clutched at his chest and splayed upon the floor, feet kicking. By the time Tong had composed himself, Bing was almost unconscious—a black gauze having enveloped his sight as a ringing overtook his hearing; a low groan passed from him.

"Bing—? Hey, you still there—? Hello—?"

After that Bing recalled nothing; not the paramedics rushing into the house, nor the short ambulance ride to Baylor Medical Center, the sirens blazing. He missed the EKG, didn't learn about the reperfusion of blood flow to his heart muscles until the next day ("An immediate percutaneous transluminal coronary angioplasty," was how the young doctor explained the process). And when he became aware in the hospital room—IV bags hanging beside his bed, needles taped at a wrist, a johnny replacing his clothing—Bing wondered if a lucid dream might be occur-

187

ring; perhaps none of it was real, he thought: the laughing with Tong, the pain, now the big nurse fiddling with an IV bag as he glanced around the room. Then all he could think to ask, at that moment, was, "What's going on here, nurse? What are you doing to me?"

"Thinning your blood," she replied.

"I don't understand."

The nurse wasn't startled by his raspy voice, his sudden stirring in the bed; she didn't even look at him. "This," she said matter-of-factly while tapping a bag, "is a clot-dissolver. We're getting a tissue plasminogen-activator and streptokinase running through you, Mister Owen."

"Doctor—Doctor Owen—"

She cocked an eyebrow, regarding Bing with a bemused expression. "It's Drain-O for the arteries," she said, half grinning. "You had a pretty tough clog, doctor."

A clog?

Bing wanted to laugh, but his stomach ached too much—so instead he returned her grin, pleased somehow by the presence of the woman. Was it her thick arms, her gray-black crewcut?

"How long have I been here?"

"At the hospital? I have no idea. In this room, about an hour."

Her masculine, no-nonsense tone?

She checked the needles in his wrist.

"Get some rest, okay? The doctor will be around in a bit to check on you."

A dyke, he figured. She's got moxie.

"Can I tell you something?" Bing asked.

"Sure."

She crossed her arms, breathing a forlorn and gentle sigh.

"This boy," Bing started, "he was walking along the sidewalk—he found this mask on the ground—a welder's mask—"

45.

TONG WAS a hero, a true lifesaver—that's what Casey told Bing: "Evidently he heard your labored breathing, understood your unresponsiveness to mean trouble, hung up and then phoned long-distance for help."

Bing looked relieved, as if this were the sort of information he should be immensely grateful to hear repeated.

"I'm fortunate, I really am. You can understand how much I owe him, Casey. He's a saint—Tong's a real gentleman."

But while remaining at the hospital for observation, Bing began resenting Tong once again. The man could do no wrong, he believed. Finding a supernova almost by accident, saving a colleague's life from hundreds of miles away.

"A true lifesaver—a hero—"

Every visitor that had come to sit beside the bed— Damien, Dr. Turman, now Casey—mentioned fantastic Tong and how lucky Bing was to be alive. To further the matter, the school newspaper joined in the praising, running a headline that made Bing wish he'd actually died instead: HOSPITALIZED FACULTY MEMBER THANKS HIS LUCKY STARS FOR ASTRONOMER'S HELP.

"I am blessed—if it weren't for Tong I surely wouldn't be here now."

Didn't they know? Should it be explained clearly? Tong nearly did me in, see. I nearly died laughing.

"The department sent an e-mail thanking him," explained Casey, who had arrived seven minutes before visiting hours concluded, slightly intoxicated, bringing copies of *Scientific American* and *National Geographic* for Bing's enjoyment.

"Good for them. I'm actually surprised—figured they'd put a price on his head for saving me."

"Now now," Casey admonished, his gin and tonic breath teasing Bing's desire for a drink.

After all, the department had sent him a large floral arrangement, a small heart-shaped pillow, and a get well card—*From all of us, with our prayers for a fast and complete recovery*—signed by his colleagues, including, to Bing's astonishment, the Trinity. "Will wonders ever cease?" he'd remarked earlier while showing Damien the card (Joy Vanderhoof's hateful signature wasn't present, of course, otherwise the gesture would have sailed into the trash).

Then more flowers were delivered, crowding the tiny bedside table, filling the room with a sweet earthy scent—dandelions from two graduate students he'd once taught; a dozen red roses from Damien, who had stopped by that afternoon with, aside from the flowers, a Sony Walkman and headphones so Bing could listen to his favorite classical radio station at night.

"Can I get you anything else?" Damien had asked when leaving.

"Yes," Bing replied, "get me a rum and coke—or get me the fuck out of here!"

He hated hospitals, despised the smell of the places, all that sterility hinting at profound sickness. And the frumpy nurses, shuffling back and forth along the corridor, in and out of rooms, like superannuated robots. And the hyper-educated doctors, speaking so clinically, saying things like, "The accumulation of cholesterol plaque caused thickening of the artery walls, narrowing the arteries—a process called atherosclerosis." He loathed the entire operation, could barely muster civility toward his own assigned physician—a kid by the looks of him: bright-blue eyes, tall, lean, clean-shaven and benign—Dr. Bagnall ("Doctor Timmy," Bing called him).

"I'd be shocked if Doctor Timmy had hair on his balls," he'd told Damien.

Dr. Bagnall reminded Bing of the man-boy that had tended Susan after her aneurysm. Same immaculate brown hair, same humorless expressions, same flat tone: "Dilatation of the blood vessel as a result of disease in the vessel wall—an abnormal blood-filled dilatation." But Bing was more patient then; perhaps because he was a young man too—or perhaps because he could leave the hospital at will. Yet he remained, day and night, talking to Susan as she lay unconscious, praying for her recovery. "We'll be going home soon," he assured her, squeezing her flimsy hand, knowing that they'd eventually return to the hospital when she gave birth.

And she did go home—but there would be no child. A week before her aneurysm they had discussed adoption: "No," she concluded. "We'll have our own baby. It's going to happen." She was wrong. When she came home there were no more attempts, no more nights or afternoons or mornings with Bing moving inside her—and, along with her desire to write and teach, the yearning for a child had vanished altogether. Like magic, Bing thought. Like a great disappearing act.

So where are you now?

(If he called she'd refuse to answer the phone.)

And why haven't you visited me?

Still, no one had asked about his wife, not Casey or Damien. Not the nurses or Dr. Timmy. But if Tong hadn't been on the other end of the line, would Susan have recognized the thump of his body hitting the floor as a sign of distress? Would she have gone from her bed or the couch to check? Would she have dared abandon her TV program and climb the stairs? A miracle, he understood, that she even opened the door for the paramedics—or had she?

No, you won't come. You won't leave the house for me.

Maybe she took him for dead. Maybe she had seen his seemingly lifeless body carted past the front door and assumed he'd already entered Heaven (the Angels had seized his spirit, had lifted him—or was it something darker, she imagined, that finally claimed his soul?). Then it would be Bing returning to her as a ghost. At last, they'd be on common ground—two specters haunting the same big house, passing through one another from time to time, free from the worries implicit in life and love and death.

But where are you now?

And where was Nick?

Of course the boy wouldn't come. That chapter was closed by meringue, by the pie assassin's ambush: if I were dead now you'd be conscience-stricken, you'd be ashamed of what you'd done.

"Well, I'm sorry to report that you're going to live a while longer," Dr. Bagnall reported, trying his best to be lighthearted.

"I know that."

Visiting hours had ended and the doctor was finishing his rounds. Bing watched television from his bed, using the remote to click around the channels, doing his best to ignore Timmy. But the doctor wouldn't leave him alone (sitting casually on the edge of the bed, pulling back the sheets some, pressing a stethoscope against the johnny, then blocking the TV screen while studying Bing's pupils).

"You know, Mister Owen, approximately one million Americans suffer a heart attack annually. About four hundred thousand of those die. Count yourself lucky."

You're a living advert for The American Heart Association, Bing wanted to tell him. "Not very lucky," he grumbled, stabbing the remote with his thumb. "Odds were in my favor."

Dr. Bagnall patted Bing's leg. "Don't be so sure of that," he said.

46.

"Four to six days," Dr. Bagnall told Bing.

Four to six days of meals brought to him (no better or worse than what Susan sometimes cooked), of flipping through the same magazines, of chatting with the big dyke nurse (her name was Karen) or the occasional visitor—of gazing blankly at the TV set that was mounted beyond reach on the wall.

"You like *Wheel of Fortune* too, huh?" Karen had said.

"Never saw it before yesterday," confessed Bing. "But it's enjoyable. I like *Jeopardy* as well—and that talk show with the fat woman."

"Oprah—maybe Rosie? Or Rosanne—?"

"I'm not sure which—one of those."

But while Bing disliked being confined to the hospital—the lack of privacy and fluorescent lights, the johnny showing his backside to the world—he was glad to be done with teaching for the semester; his heart attack, in a way, had liberated him from that tedious chore. Sweet of Casey, he thought, taking over my class and office hours. And those spring students—not such a bad bunch, not quite like the fall brats—just today they had sent him a get well card, along with some lilacs for the bed-side table. Now summer had arrived months ahead of schedule, and a much needed rest was in order, even if it began in a hospital bed.

Four to six days—

Still, he longed for a drink (a glass of wine, maybe a pint of Ten High, something potent to help pass the hours); then perhaps he wouldn't have to think anymore (You won't come, Susan—and Nick—), or ponder hospitals or faulty arteries—or, as was the case now, Marc: Bing had last seen him in a comparable bed, IV's in the wrists, unconscious, breathing with the aid of a respirator. The boy's head was so swollen and bruised that his features weren't fully recog-

193

nizable (lips all purple and damaged, surely not the lips that once offered such fervent kisses); a frightful and distancing sight, keeping Bing from sitting beside him, from holding his hand and speaking to him like he'd done for Susan. Of course, Marc's parents and older brother were usually present, and any sign of affection would likely have been frowned upon (who was this youngish professor so concerned about their son's plight?). That inconsolable family—did they even fathom Marc's nature or comprehend the boy's fondness for Bing (the skin his lips had sucked, the places his hands had stroked)? Did they know that with the inevitable flip of a switch, the yank of a plug, the only lover Bing ever treasured would simply cease to be? But then again no one knew. Nothing was more apparent than this: a student had been struck by a car while riding his bicycle through an intersection, and, hardly surprising to his colleagues and acquaintances, Bing was visibly saddened by the accident.

"He was a very nice kid, it's a shame."

"A good student, I recall."

"Yes, a very good student."

No one saw the grief he carried—the tears that erupted as he drove home from teaching, the anger that pounded his fists against the steering wheel. No one knew that while Marc functioned on the respirator, Bing went to his apartment, unlocking the door with a spare key—and stayed there for hours, weeping aloud, pressing his face into the boy's pillow, rifling through his dirty clothes basket for T-shirts and underwear, clutching at anything which retained a trace or smell of him. And then, on the very day Marc stopped breathing, Bing stole once more into that apartment, gathering the notes and letters he had signed (*As always, with love—Bing*), retrieving the coffee cup Marc had put aside for his use—and a few articles of the boy's clothing that were folded carefully and kept hidden like sacred garments.

But he didn't attend the funeral, couldn't bring himself to stand amongst the sorrowful. Yet he mourned all the same, getting lost in what he understood as his own quiet tragedy. Then how comforting the bottle became, how much like an agreeable protector—and when slipping into drunkenness, he felt closer to Marc, could somehow sense his presence. In the beginning, the pain of losing him was reason enough for the glass to be refilled, the second bottle uncorked, the seal on a bourbon pint cracked; until—at last—there was no pain at all, just more bottles and fitful nights and the distractions of work—and Susan again.

Eventually the memories of anxious sex on warm afternoons and of Marc's receptive body—the taut chest with hair around the navel, the muscular thighs flexing—grew into a sustaining fantasy. Only later, as the want for another became overwhelming, did Bing hopelessly seek out someone else. By then he was too old for the fashionable dance clubs, and encounters with men his own age seemed a depressing pursuit. But there was the bathroom in the library basement. How often did he frequent the place in vain? How many times did he loiter before a urinal, fly undone, waiting for contact? And when the moment finally arrived (a nervous black kid had paused beside him with an erection, two fingers caressing his testicles), Bing fled the bathroom in disgust, feeling somewhat noble in not succumbing to what he desired most: a cock sliding into his mouth, then the sperm of a young man splashing across his tongue. Thank God for HIV, he thought—for the fear of the virus held his darkest cravings at bay.

So it was always back home to Susan, to their separate worlds. How Bing hated not longing for her the same way as he longed for a dead boy—or how he never needed her as much as the bottles standing on the wet bar, or the drinks poured at Eric's. And how now—reclining in that hospital bed, the TV showing Vanna White turning letters—he wanted his veins flushed with red wine. He wanted IV's supplying a fine merlot, the curtains drawn, and Karen rubbing at his shoulders until he slept. He wanted everything made indistinct and nearly forgotten. Was that asking too much?

47.

SLEEP OVERTOOK Bing so easily now. Television was like a drug, he decided. Every evening his eyelids became heavy, and he would begin dozing in the middle of the news or a sitcom, the remote sliding through lax fingers. Twice visitors came (Dr. Turman and then the hospital chaplain, a jovial man who laughed too readily) only to find him snoring in his bed, head propped and tilted to one side on the pillow, while the TV continued playing.

But the sudden drowsiness felt welcome; a kind of fatigue that was at once warming and relentlessly acute. Then Bing would wake at dawn, refreshed and clearheaded, ready for breakfast, the newspaper, a little small talk with whichever nurse was on duty. Later he'd take supervised walks up and down and around the hospital corridors, encountering more enfeebled patients (a wheelchair-bound elderly man with watery gray eyes, the left side of his body paralyzed; a teenage girl missing her right foot, miserably going forward on crutches); Bing passed them by without as much as a nod: "Christ, it's like doing laps at the Special Olympics," he told Mr. Agawa, the handsome Asian orderly who accompanied him each morning.

"Well, tomorrow we'll do three laps," Mr. Agawa said.

"How about four?"

"Okay, four then. If you want."

Everyday his activity was increased, every night he slept deeply. And Dr. Bagnall continually reminded Bing that exercise was an important ingredient in preventing another heart attack. "Before you're discharged," the doctor explained, "you'll be prescribed activity regimens for when you return home."

Home.

By the fourth day Bing no longer wished to leave. He enjoyed all the attention, the company of Mr. Agawa and

Nurse Karen—even the infamous hospital cooking ("You think I could get some wine or a beer with my dinner," he half joked). Yet the days were sluggish, lethargic at best, and he suspected the exercise with Mr. Agawa fueled the evening fatigue; some nights he slept fourteen hours, other nights it was between ten and twelve—and always he awoke with a faint anxiety troubling his mind: Did Pussy have enough food? Water? And what was Susan doing? Where was she?

You won't come.

Though on the night prior to his discharge she did come—arriving with Nick an hour or so before visiting hours concluded. But because he had already drifted off, had become lost within that dreamless and impenetrable sleep, Bing was unaware of the visitation. Still, they remained—Nick leaning against a wall, Susan sitting near the bedside table—hoping he might possibly stir, if just for a moment.

Only later did Bing learn that Nick had first stopped by the house to inquire about his condition. And, miracle of miracles, Susan had answered the door, gazing at the boy with searching and frightened eyes; as if she expected some awful news from him, for Nick to say, "I'm sorry, but Professor Owen is dead." Then it became clear to the boy: No one had called her, no one had come by. How puzzling to discover—standing there in the doorway, her arms dangling at her sides—that Susan didn't know where the paramedics had taken her husband. She didn't know who to call, she didn't know where to go—but Nick did.

"Can you take me?" Susan asked.

"Yes, of course."

"Thank you."

So they arrived together—Susan bringing nothing except her *Living Bible*; Nick holding a handmade card fashioned out of pink construction paper—embellished by white stars, blue half-moons, a yellow sun bearing two round eyes and a smile—which, when found the following morning, filled Bing with cheer and relief (the cover offered a balanced quote from Jessamyn West—*It is easy to forgive others their mistakes. It takes more gut and gumption to forgive them for having witnessed your own*; the inside read: *Bing, hope you're feeling better and doing well. Your friend, Nick*). And that night, once Nurse Karen had entered the room and explained in hushed words that visiting hours were over, Nick glanced at Susan, saying, "We'll come back tomorrow, if you want."

Susan stared at him, then Karen. She bit her lip, shaking her head some. "I'll be staying," she said.

"Unfortunately," Karen said, "unless you're immediate family it's not allowed."

Susan absently turned a page.

Nick crossed his arms.

The nurse sighed, waiting for the pair to gather up and go. Her glances were serious and wary: Don't you people understand? But Nick and Susan didn't move—she in the chair with her bible, him peeking glimpses at the television—as if contemplating a standoff.

"It's hospital policy, you know. I don't have any say in the matter."

"Well, she's pretty immediate," Nick told Karen.

"Oh—?"

"She's his wife."

The nurse shrugged passively. "I see," she said, then considered having a foldaway rolled into the room: "I suppose we can—"

But Susan appeared untroubled and resigned in the chair. Her eyes lowered to the book. She began underlining text with an index finger. Her expression was impassive, making clear her lack of interest in the environs, even as the TV showed an elephant running amok at a circus in Ohio.

"Never mind," Karen concluded. "Just let me know if you need anything. I'll check in from time to time."

So after Nick left (his agile body receding down the long and empty corridor, seeming to illuminate every so often as he crossed beneath fluorescent lights), after Dr. Bagnall finished his evening rounds ("It's not unusual for a patient to sleep so soundly, especially considering the medication he's on"), Susan shut her bible, keeping it in her lap. She shifted in the chair, gazing upward at the TV, and exhaled a steady breath.

I am here.

Soon she reached for the remote, extricating it gingerly from her husband's grasp. Then, throughout the night, she maintained her vigil, sitting in that chair beside his bed, going from channel to channel—ABC, NBC, CBS, CNN, CBN—as the hospital hibernated, lulled by the electrical drone of its own internal oscillations.

When Bing awoke at dawn, he saw that the television was still on with the sound turned low. So he lay there on his side, not yet willing to sit upright, watching the screen (an early morning cartoon: Daffy Duck and Bugs Bunny being chased by a witch inside a haunted house). It wasn't until Susan placed a hand gently on his wrist that he realized her presence—was there reproachfulness in his eyes as he turned to see her, or a trace of that morning anxiety?—and so it was as if she had suddenly emerged from nowhere, had perhaps passed into the room through a wall. Now she was standing beside the bed, wrapping her fingers around his wrist.

"I'm here—"

How propitious. But he couldn't speak, couldn't find his voice. And looking into her dark reflective eyes Bing caught sight of himself—mouth hanging open, brow wrinkled in confusion, hair a mess. As she sat upon the edge of the bed, his chest began convulsing, his hands trembling. But she wasn't startled by the spasms now seizing him, wasn't surprised by the crippling fit, the onset of which closed his eyes—no tears would spring forth, no sobs would escape—

leaving his mouth gaped, as if he were attempting a tortured lament that had no audible or known sound. So she would simply take him, would bring him to her breast and hold him there. How much bigger she seemed just then—how benevolent and large she was, cradling such a small and brittle man, saying only to him, "I'm here, I'm here—"

SUSAN

48.

Tell me what it is you know.
Is it that I have no life with him?
That I am not his heart's want?
But you see he gave me a home,
even if it were his as well,
and not as a gift or offering,
but as a clandestine sanctuary
where the rooms became a refuge
in which I could disappear within
and be saved from remembering.
So being away from our house now
fosters an agitation, making me like a hiker
hurrying in the woods at dusk,
worried of becoming lost in darkness.
Or afraid of what darkness might bring.

Explain again what is so important:
I desire to be whole and deserving
as she who has survived the days
with herself completed,
with her troubled soul resolving
that bargain we proclaim as faith.
Only then I can return to my past
and recall with the stinging clarity
of a slapped cheek
what exactly he implied
while uttering, "I love you so much."

So what you know
is that he wasn't a cruel man,
nor was he purely faulty in his ways;

he never struck out or hit.
And who hasn't carried
his kind of longing or discontent?
And what should be apparent
is that he did love someone;
perhaps it was only me,
perhaps it was others.
But he did love,
for whatever love is
or is worth.

Now explain it once again
what it was you thought important.
Were you going to tell me
that all eventually touches all,
everything becoming inseparable?
Or was it just that,
like the stars above
and the earth below,
you comprehended human affection
as a most confounding and mystifying thing?

EPILOGUE

AN *INSUBSTANTIAL* lunch, as usual.

As usual, a tossed salad with a low-fat Ranch dressing, tomato soup, and a glass of peach-flavored iced tea. For dessert: an aspirin tablet, good for the heart and good for the head.

Then how vigorous Bing felt when standing before his graduate students, not at all indolent, no, not even tardy. And a week ago, at the fall faculty luncheon, he mingled with a glass of water in hand, smiling while engaging his associates, standing amongst the Trinity for a group photograph of the Astronomy Department—the faggot, Jew, and royal cunt apparently pleased by his return to form (the Big Bing had reduced to a slender singularity during the summer, had watched his dietary fat and lowered his serum cholesterol).

"Christ, you're looking great."

"Well, thank you."

"Nice to have you with us, Bing. We were pretty worried about you there for a while."

"Thought we almost lost you."

So who despised him now? Who could complain after seeing him so agreeable and healthy and trim? Only Joy Vanderhoof, he imagined—but, with Cosmology and Astrophysics back on his fall plate, Theoretical Astrophysics and Theories of Space-Time in the spring, Bing couldn't care less: a bitch is a bitch is a bitch is a—

"Hello, Joy," he had said amiably when encountering her at the luncheon.

"Professor Owen," was her terse response.

No matter, he figured today. No matter as he wandered across campus, freed from his late afternoon class. The *declining sun cast his long shadow in front of him—further ahead Herbert R. Moss' statue loomed. And where exactly had he been ambushed? Where was the spot? Alongside the tomb, underneath Moss' icy stare?*

No matter.

He had forgiven Nick, Nick had forgiven him. They had made their peace modestly enough, though neither brought up the events which forged the rift in the friendship—even as they met for coffee on a hot July night, as they sat in a booth at House of Pies and, for the first and only time since the regretful groping, spoke to one another—just small talk, nothing too interesting (Nick's recent attempt at fiction, the article Bing planned on writing about self-reproducing cosmos). Then they had hugged afterwards, embracing in the parking lot before going separate ways. Or Nick hugged Bing, albeit quickly, saying, "Take care of yourself."

"You too," he replied. "Be careful."

And that was that.

The boy had not seen him again, nor had he called or stopped by the house or, as promised, sent along a copy of his short story (something about two brothers finding a loaded handgun in an alley trash can). But Bing had seen him; he had spotted Nick three days ago while crossing the quad, spying the boy as he lay shirtless on the grass. And what a beautiful day it was—clear with a hard blue sky, the summer torridness having finally abated—such a perfect day for throwing a football around, for reading a book outdoors—or sunbathing. And Nick: resting beside another shirtless boy, an Asian kid, both wearing sunglasses and letting the rays warm their narrow chests; what casual intimacy, Bing thought, what luxury of youth. Two boys so comfortable with each other, so at ease upon the grass together—like white dwarfs, he envisioned, compact and insulated, feeding off their own heat (not like me, not like this red giant of a man—my heat flux wishes to waylay them, to distend outward and engulf those lesser stars in my fiery vacuum). Better to walk on, he concluded, and never look back. Better to continue forward on that fine day, whistling a tune while somehow sensing the storm that would roar in from the Gulf before midnight—a downpour that would flood the bayous and streets, turning stalled cars into ineffective boats.

But today—the storm having come and gone, its havoc already forgotten—how lovely the world seemed to Bing as he took a patio table at Eric's Rotisserie. And with oaks branching out, shading the nearby sidewalk, he found himself whistling once more. Even in the evening, Moss was teeming with fresh faces, and Bing felt uncanny and sharp, as new and alive as the young people moving along on the sidewalk. With his hair combed neatly, swept over the bald spot on his shiny scalp, his bow tie pressing at his throat, he folded his hands in his lap—the very vision of a self-assured and purposeful academic—gazing at the young men roaming in various directions, off to the library or to dinner, heading for walkways that ran alongside the ivy-covered buildings, a few pausing together beneath the oaks. Smooth skin and tanned necks sheltered under clustered leaves. Every single one beyond his reach.

"Our wine list?" the waitress asked.

"No, not today," Bing said, ignoring the menu she held out for him. "I'll just have water."

"Are you expecting anyone else? Should I leave a menu?"

"No," he answered, "and no."

And soon, while sipping his glass of water, Bing would toast the new students and the Trinity and the squirrel that scampered about the patio. Not as good as wine, he thought. Not as satisfying as a fine merlot. But he would toast the lumbering city anyway, the skyscrapers, the university, the riddles of the heavens and of the earth— until, the glass at last emptied, he would rise steadily from the table and start home.